P9-DKF-937

That Thing We Call a Heart

That Thing We Call a Heart

SHEBA KARIM

HARPER TEEN
An Imprint of HarperCollins*Publishers*

HarperTeen is an imprint of HarperCollins Publishers.

That Thing We Call a Heart

www.epicreads.com
Library of Congress Control Number: 2016949962
ISBN 978-0-06-244570-4
Typography by Erin Fitzsimmons
17 18 19 20 21 PC/LSCH 10 9 8 7 6 5 4 3 2 1

First Edition

This book is dedicated to my dear friend Abeer Hoque
and all the other "Muslims like us."

That Thing We Call a Heart

I.

The Desert of Loneliness

One

"CHECK OUT THE PIG!"

Lincoln Prep's senior class, minus Farah, did a 180 toward the backyard, where an entire roasted pig sat on top of an ornate silver platter, nestled amid pineapple and cherry tomato skewers. The pig was wearing a lei of silk flowers and aviator sunglasses, a cigar dangling precariously from its lips.

With a whoop, Ryan D'Ambrosio III leaped out of the pool, zigzagging through the crowd. Waving a bamboo torch in one hand, he posed with the pig, smiling broadly as the senior paparazzi whipped out their phones to take a photo of their dripping demigod. As the flashes went off, Natasha St. Clair kicked off her stilettos and ran over to Ryan, climbing onto his back.

Ryan stole the cigar from the pig and handed it to Natasha,

who stuck it in her mouth.

"His abs are unreal," Danny said.

"I bet he has a small dick," Ian retorted.

"Shut it," Danny replied. "Don't kill my Ryan fantasy."

"You have a Ryan fantasy?" I said. "Don't you think he's homophobic?"

"Oh, he is," Danny agreed, "until our eyes meet in the locker room shower and his towel slips off to reveal his huge—"

As Ian made a gagging sound, Ryan yelled,"Who wants first dibs at the pig?" He dashed through the crowd, holding the torch high like an Olympian, Natasha perched on his shoulders, her tanned thighs squeezing his neck, pumping her fist as together they chanted, "Pig pig pig pig."

If Farah were here, she would be disgusted, partly because like most Muslims she thought pigs were gross, but mostly because she couldn't stand Ryan or Natasha. Ryan drove a silver BMW convertible with a bumper sticker that said "Don't Spread My Wealth, Spread My Work Ethic." He was the beautiful captain of our nationally ranked lacrosse team, and though his jokes were predictably juvenile, when he held the door open with his winning smile and said, "After you," you'd have to be either cold-blooded or as principled as Farah not to flutter a little.

"Bermuda, Bahama, come on pretty mama . . ."

"That's the fifth time this song has played," Danny complained. "I know this is a luau but *come on*. Ian, do something."

"Fine," Ian said, rolling up his T-shirt sleeves. "Quick,

Shabnam, give me a song."

"'Sit Down. Stand Up,'" I said. "Radiohead."

"I was thinking more Beyoncé," Danny protested, but Ian had already sprinted away.

I scooped out what remained of my watermelon Jell-O shot, sucking it off my finger. Natasha had started squealing: Ryan was threatening to toss her into the pool.

Natasha St. Clair's luau was an annual event, the party of the season. It was normally the domain of the popular kids, but, this being our final year at Lincoln Prep, Natasha had magnanimously handed out custom-made, pig-shaped paper invites to the entire class. If Farah and I were still best friends, tomorrow we'd have a recap session in which we'd laugh our asses off making fun of Ryan and Natasha and pretty much everything about this party.

The Beach Boys were silenced mid-verse, and replaced by my favorite band. I loved the energy of "Sit Down. Stand Up," the way the song built, the way it moved, how if you closed your eyes and really listened you could feel it shuddering inside your veins. I wanted to dance but was too self-conscious to do anything more than sway a little.

As the song was about to hit its climax, Natasha pulled the plug.

"Attention!" she cried. "Everyone inside the house, now!"

As we followed the herd, Danny said, "I hope the cops aren't here."

"Nah," Ian said. "And even if they were, her dad just donated twenty thousand dollars to the local police department."

"How do you know?" Danny asked.

"I heard her bragging about it in photo lab."

After we'd gathered in the living room, Natasha climbed onto the coffee table, a huge slab of white marble perched atop a ball and triangle. She fluffed out her hula skirt and adjusted her gold-sequined bikini. Like Ryan, her abs were also unreal.

"Now listen up, y'all," she said. We were in New Jersey, but Natasha's mother was a former Southern beauty queen; there was a framed photo of her on the wall behind Natasha, a severe blonde wearing a glittering, pointy crown.

"I want all of the girls to line up against the wall," Natasha continued, "and the boys to line up across from them."

No one moved.

"Come on, people," Natasha cried. "You gotta play to stay."

As the boys and girls began to split into their respective lines, Ian raised his hand.

"Does sexual preference factor at all in line selection?"

"If you have a cock, go there," Natasha barked, gesturing with her thumb at the guys lining up behind her. "No cock, over there."

"Well, that's one way of dividing the world," Ian muttered.

Natasha held up a Louis Vuitton bag that was even wider than her hula skirt. "Now, I want all the girls to put their cell phones inside here," she declared. "Come on, ladies, don't be scared.

Y'all might end up having the best night of your life."

As the non-popular among us exchanged wary glances, the popular girls, who were clustered at the other end of the line, began, one by one, to relinquish their phones to the almighty Natasha.

I glanced at my phone: 10:02 p.m. There was still enough time to play this stupid game and have Ian drop me home before my 11:00 p.m. curfew. If Farah had deigned to come to the luau, this was when she'd get the hell out. I should have done the same, but instead, I tossed my phone into the Louis Vuitton abyss, hoping the outcome would be "yes, in fact the best night of your life" rather than "abject humiliation in front of the entire senior class."

Having assumed control of the girls' phones, Natasha moved on to the boys, instructing each of them to pick a phone from the bag and, without looking, put it in their pocket.

Guessing this was some sort of girl-boy matchup, I went down the line, counting friendly faces. If it was Ian or Danny, I was safe. Paul, too, and Julio. They wouldn't obey Natasha's orders if it meant embarrassing me. At least, I didn't think so.

Once every boy had a phone, Natasha walked up and down between the two lines, a captain instructing us on our mission. "This game is called Ten Minutes. The point is to spend ten minutes together, anywhere—a room, a bathroom, underneath a tree, as long as it's only the two of you. A closet works, too. Once everyone is paired up, you have one minute to find your hideout. I'll blow a whistle ten minutes later, though you can stay longer if you want."

Some guests began to grumble, disappointed that this was nothing more than a technologically advanced version of Seven Minutes in Heaven, but Natasha silenced them with an over-the-head clap. Her pits were insanely smooth, like no hair dared grow there. We attended the same school, but her life was a different country: sailboats, ski trips, country clubs, armpits you could stick right in someone's face and not be ashamed.

"Get your minds out of the gutter!" Natasha admonished us. "You can spend your ten minutes talking, or singing, or doing body shots, whatever. Feel free to document your time together—#10minutesinheaven. Other than that, there are no rules."

Except, of course, for the rule that we had to spend ten minutes in close proximity.

Amelia handed Natasha an old-school white cordless phone, with a show of solemnity, like someone was about to get kicked off the island.

"Any volunteers to go first?" Natasha asked.

"Me!" Amelia cried, jumping back into line with cheerleader enthusiasm. Natasha returned the phone, and Amelia dialed her own number. It rang inside the pocket of Oliver, another popular kid, which made me suspect the game was rigged, at least until the next volunteer, a popular girl named Kate, got paired up with Noah, a gamer geek.

When it was my turn, I wished for Danny and Ian, hoping to spend my ten minutes talking about how lame this luau was.

But it wasn't Danny or Ian who pulled my phone out of his pocket.

It was Ryan D'Ambrosio III.

"Pair up!" Natasha cried with a smirk.

As I stepped forward, I could feel the jealous stares of the other girls and Danny, like darts aimed at my spine. In school, I'd been a disregarded entity until I became friends with Farah, and I'd certainly never been an object of envy. As hormonally exciting as it was to stand within inches of a nearly naked, blue-eyed, perfectly chiseled Ryan, it was also terrifying. I'd inherited not only my father's round face, curly hair, and bushy eyebrows that demanded frequent threading, but also a bit of his awkwardness. I was fine with people I knew, but socializing with strangers made me nervous, especially if I wanted to make a good impression. A knot would form in the space between my stomach and my heart; I'd sweat a little and and blurt out something ridiculous, or long-winded, or both.

Ryan wasn't a stranger, exactly, but the only things I'd ever said to him were "Thank you," the two times he'd held the door open for me, and "Excuse me," the time I'd bumped into him outside the cafeteria. I doubted he even knew who I was.

"I guess tonight's the best night of your life," Ryan informed me as he returned my phone, "because I've got a surprise for us."

Then he winked.

A surprise? For us? I pinched my lips together, determined not to say anything stupid, wondering what I would do if it involved something sexual. Ryan had been breaking hearts since kindergarten, and I'd only kissed two boys in my life—the first because of Spin the Bottle, the second Ian, because he felt sorry for me that I'd only kissed one guy.

I knew I shouldn't even be *nice* to Ryan, much less kiss him, but what chance did my moral compass have against curiosity, teenage hormones, a watermelon Jell-O shot, and the hottest boy in school?

Natasha, who was apparently exempt from the game, blew a whistle. "Everyone find a spot!" she ordered.

"Let's go!" Ryan said.

I followed him up the grand, curving staircase to the end of the hallway. Ryan pushed open a pair of double doors flanked by pillars and entered the master bedroom suite, locking the door after I stepped inside. The centerpiece of the room was a circular bed, over which hung a recent portrait of Natasha's mother, even blonder than in her beauty queen days. She wore a slightly strained expression, like her pearl choker was cutting off her oxygen. She seemed even more intimidating than her daughter, so I was glad when Ryan headed into the bathroom. It was larger than my room at home, featuring his-and-her sinks, a steam shower, a green marble Jacuzzi, and a dressing area with a gilded mirror.

Ryan leaned over a sink and splashed his face, droplets of

water flying as he tossed his head.

"You sat a few desks in front of me in econ class last year," he said, looking at me in the mirror. "I remember your hair."

My hand flew to my curls. They were, for better or worse, my most memorable attribute. "They're my dad's," I said. "I mean, I get my hair from my dad. He's bald now, though. Well, not totally, he's got a ring, like Mr. Burns, you know, from *The Simpsons*."

Ryan was nodding slowly, probably assessing the stability of my mental state. The back of my neck was slick with sweat. Why couldn't I keep my mouth shut?

"You're friends with the Muslim chick," he said.

"Not anymore." I immediately hated myself for saying this. Except it was sort of true.

"Hair makes a woman," he proclaimed.

If that was the case, then what did my hair make me?

Ryan whirled around. "Let's pop this baby!"

I stepped back in alarm as he ran across the bathroom and jumped into the Jacuzzi. A moment later, he proudly held up a bottle of champagne. "Dom," he said. "Nats gave me a heads-up about the game so I stole a bottle of the good stuff from her parents' bar and stashed it in the hot tub."

"Wow," I said, because he clearly expected praise.

Ryan leaned back, stretching his sculpted arms along the tub's scalloped edge. "You coming in or what?"

There was no water in the tub so I figured I could enter fully clothed. With a deep breath, I abandoned my post at the doorway and joined him. Ryan braced the bottle between his thighs and uncorked it, letting out a gleeful hoot as it popped.

"After you," he said.

If Farah were here, she'd say something like, "No, assholes first," and throw the champagne in his face.

But I'd never had champagne, I'd never sat in a Jacuzzi, I'd never been alone with a boy this hot.

Plus, he was actually being pretty nice. He'd even remembered me.

I took a swig.

Champagne was good.

"What are you?" Ryan asked. "Sri Lankan?"

"No," I said, impressed that he'd referenced one of the lesser known countries from the subcontinent.

"I dated a Sri Lankan girl for a while. She had this incredible hair, jet-black and down to her butt. It smelled like coconuts."

I wondered if this was offensive but after my second swig decided it was more a statement of fact. I returned the bottle but he set it aside and began inching forward. It wasn't until his face was right in front of mine that I realized he was going to kiss me.

Ryan D'Ambrosio III thought I was good enough to kiss.

He tasted like beer and Vaseline, and kissing him wasn't as great as I'd hoped. I couldn't appreciate his beauty when my eyes were closed but it was too weird to keep them open. When he put his tongue inside me, I felt like it was taking up too much of my mouth. When I pushed back with my own tongue, it was more in self-defense than passion. My conscience chastised me, emboldened.

What the hell, it said. *Do you not remember what he did?*

Wait, I insisted. *This kiss could get better.*

The whistle blew, announcing the end of ten minutes. Ryan pulled away, chugged the champagne.

"Later," he said, wiping his mouth with the back of his hand and stepping out of the tub. "You know what—you should have this," he said, presenting me with the nearly empty bottle, like a consolation prize.

I stayed in the Jacuzzi for a few minutes, bruised by his sudden exit. For both of us, these ten minutes had been a curious departure from the norm, except that when the whistle blew I'd wanted to kiss some more, and he'd wanted to return to the norm, and his real friends, and the women he should really be kissing.

I'd forsaken my principles for a hot tub and champagne.

If Farah found out, she'd kill me. But who cared what she thought?

That was when it occurred to me that I might have kissed Ryan to spite her, because I was upset she'd ended our friendship, and because I missed her so much.

What was wrong with me?

I was actually relieved that the kiss with Ryan sucked. Because if it had been hot, and I'd been into it, I would have felt even more guilty, and confused.

Two

"WHAT ARE YOU WEARING?" my mother whispered as I walked into the kitchen in my pajamas. "Your great-uncle is here! Didn't you see the *shalwar kameez* I left on your chair? Please go change. And comb your hair. And put on a bra! And go sit at the table and talk to him because you know your father isn't."

I didn't bother arguing; my mother always freaked out when we had guests because she wanted badly for them to have a lovely time in spite of her uninterested daughter and disinterested husband.

The bathroom contained evidence of my mysterious great-uncle's early morning arrival; the toilet seat was up, and there was a gray pube-like hair in the sink. I decided if my great-uncle didn't have to put the toilet seat down, I didn't have to wear a *shalwar kameez*, and returned downstairs in jeans and a T-shirt.

My great-uncle was sitting opposite my father at the dining table. His wiry gray bush of a beard covered half his face, extending several inches beyond his jaw at a forward angle. He had a dent in the center of his forehead, a mark of piety caused by spending so much time in prostration during prayer. He was wearing a starched, spotless white *shalwar kameez*, a black vest, and sandals with polished leather straps. Wrap a turban around his head and he could easily have passed for a very meticulously dressed member of the Pakistani Taliban.

"*As'salaam alaikum*," I greeted him, uncertain of what to call him. He was technically my dad's father's cousin, and in Urdu practically every relative has their own honorific.

"*Wa'alaikum salaam*." My great-uncle held up the fancy china teapot my mother reserved for guests. "Will you take some chai?"

"Okay," I said, sitting down next to my father. My great-uncle smiled at me as he passed me my tea, as though he wasn't secretly judging me for exposing three quarters of my arms.

My father was hidden behind the *New York Times*, making disapproving grunts as he read. He was antisocial and often socially awkward; he wasn't one for pleasantries, though he did have the occasional, uncanny ability to say exactly the wrong thing at the wrong time. There were, however, certain things he liked to wax on about, namely politics and Urdu poetry. He could talk math, too, which to him was its own kind of poetry, but thankfully didn't bother with us because we wouldn't understand. No doubt it was my mother who insisted his uncle stay over, as my father didn't extend invitations. He wouldn't even talk to his own sister if my mother didn't stick the phone to his ear once a month. And he didn't talk to me much, which was fine, because I had no interest in politics or Urdu poetry.

"And they call this a liberal newspaper," my father said to himself, scooping up some cumin-fried potatoes with his fingers.

My great-uncle looked at me. I could tell he was confused by my father's behavior. He obviously didn't know him well.

When my father wasn't at the university, or locked in his study, he spent 50 percent of his waking hours lost in thought, and 50 percent talking back to the news. Sometimes he would talk at us. Once in a while, he'd join in on a conversation between my mother and me, usually with non sequiturs.

"Dad's a mathematician. They're kinda weird," I explained to my great-uncle, in case he didn't know.

"Shabnam!" my mother admonished, entering the room with a plate of eggs.

"What?" I said. "It's true." I'd gone to one of my father's department parties a few years ago. Aside from an effusive Trinidadian woman and a man with a long braid who knew some cool card tricks, they were an awkward bunch. Half the people didn't look at you when they talked, a few of them barely talked, a few barely spoke English, and one guy literally looked like he'd escaped from an insane asylum. Turned out he was the chair of the department. They all seemed very comfortable together, though, communicating in a math language that was beyond the comprehension of us mere mortals.

Behind the paper, my father belched.

"More omelet?" my mother asked my great-uncle, heaping some onto his plate without waiting for a response.

My great-uncle took a small bite of the omelet and started to cough.

My mother wrinkled her forehead. "Too many green chilies?" she asked. "Let me go make another."

"No, please, sit down. You've already worked so hard. Relax, eat," he insisted, but he clearly didn't know my mother well either.

I helped myself to some omelet, hoping food would ease my hangover—after Ryan left me, I'd finished his Dom backwash. My great-uncle picked up the *tasbih*—the Muslim rosary—lying next to his plate. My mother had one but his was nicer, the stone beads a deep orange in color, the tassel made of delicate silver chains, each chain ending in a tiny orange bead ornamented with finely wrought silver.

He began to pray, his lips forming silent words as the beads moved through his fingers.

My mother returned, removing my great-uncle's plate and replacing it with a less spicy omelet.

"Thank you," my great-uncle said. At least he was polite.

"But if you don't mind, I'll only have chai and biscuits now, and eat after my morning walk."

"Would you like more biscuits? We have Marie biscuits."

"No, I'll walk now," he said.

"Of course," my mother said. "We have a lovely park down the hill, but it's about a twenty-minute walk, and then you have to walk back uphill."

"That's all right," he said. "I'd probably get lost."

"Shabnam could take you."

I glared at my mother. There was no way I was going to take a morning stroll through our neighborhood with a guy who was a turban away from scary mullah.

"That's all right," my great-uncle said. "I'll walk down the street and come back."

Phew. After he left, my mother said, "Shabnam, I want you to take Chotay Dada to the mall."

Chotay Dada translated into "little grandfather." So that was what I was supposed to call him. Both of my grandfathers died before I could remember them, but he was a poor substitute. Grandfathers were supposed to be cuddly, good-humored, gift-bearing—not look like they might deliver a sermon that ended with "Death to America."

"Take him to the Apple store at Fifty Oaks," my mother continued. Fifty Oaks was the most upscale mall in our area. "He wants to buy an iPad for his granddaughter in Cleveland."

"Why can't he go when he's in Cleveland?"

"Because he wants to buy it here. Don't argue with me. His flight is tonight, so you have to be back by five at the latest."

"Why can't Dad take him?" I demanded. "It's his uncle."

My mother rarely became angry. Instead, she turned pale and wide-eyed, a damsel in distress. If you continued to argue, the rims of her sweet, fragile brown eyes would dampen with tears, and the sight of her, looking like a lovely wounded gazelle, would compel you to cease and desist.

"Fine," I muttered.

My mother smiled, ruffling my hair. "Thank you, *beta*. Now come help me wash the dishes."

I followed my mother through the living room, where she drew back the drapes to check on our guest. Chotay Dada was walking down the sidewalk, the prayer beads dangling from his hand.

"Look at him," she said. "Over eighty years old but in better health than your father."

"I hope none of our neighbors see him and call the FBI."

"Be nice to him, Shabu. He's had a difficult year. His wife died, and his son told me he's been thinking a lot about what happened to him during Partition."

"Really?" I said. We'd just read about the Partition of India into India and Pakistan in history class. "What happened to him during Partition?"

"I don't know. It's not the sort of thing you ask. It's too unpleasant a subject."

My mother didn't talk about unpleasant subjects.

"Can you change into a more modest T-shirt before going to the mall?" she asked.

"Can he change into normal clothes before going to the mall?" I replied.

"You shouldn't be ashamed of who you are," my mother said.

Except Chotay Dada and I had nothing in common. Last night, while I'd been left in a Jacuzzi clutching a bottle of Dom, he'd probably been prostrate on a prayer rug clutching his *tasbih*.

Annoyed by my mother's request for me to wear modest clothing, I'd put on a turtleneck, which was a dumb idea because it was ninety degrees out and the mall parking lot was full. By the time Chotay Dada and I reached the entrance, sweat was streaming down my face, forming little eddies in my sideburns. Chotay Dada, of course, was unchanged, the prayer beads still in his right hand.

I was certain everyone was going to stare at him, so once we entered the mall I walked a few feet ahead, refusing to focus on anyone or anything, determined to get to Apple and then get the hell out.

Except Chotay Dada quickened his pace and caught up with me. If I walked ahead of him now it would be supremely rude, so instead I shifted a few steps sideways. That was when I saw Natasha and Amelia striding toward us, dressed in tight tank tops and denim miniskirts, Natasha sipping on a giant smoothie, swinging a diamond peace sign key chain around her finger.

Panicked by the possibility of the two of them seeing me with Chotay Dada, I ducked into the closest store.

The store happened to be a Victoria's Secret. On one hand, this was awesome because I doubted Chotay Dada would follow me inside; on the other, I'd run into a lingerie store in front of my religious great-uncle. I glanced over my shoulder. He'd moved to a bench across from the store, the beads moving through his fingers, waiting for me to return. As they walked past him, Natasha and Amelia nudged each other, Natasha whispering something that made Amelia snicker. I wanted to stay long enough to make sure they were gone, but I couldn't peruse a selection of lingerie while Chotay Dada was watching, so I headed to a display of perfumes and sniffed a few with feigned interest.

"Do you like that one?"

On the other side of the perfume display was a cute guy with sharp cheekbones and an even sharper jaw, the angular intensity of his face balanced by the soft warmth of his hazel eyes, the kind you had to stare at to figure out what color they were exactly. He had a pale scar running in a jagged diagonal across the back of his right hand. It was a little jarring when you first noticed it, but also strangely beautiful.

"Huh?" I said, pulling at my turtleneck and wishing that for once I could meet someone cute and not be sweaty and nervous.

"That perfume," he explained, gesturing at the heart-shaped bottle in my hand. "I have this gift card and thought I'd buy something for my aunt. Do you like it?"

"I don't really like perfume," I said.

"Then why are you smelling all of them?"

I had no good answer to this, so instead I blurted, "You have a very interesting scar."

He was taken aback for a second, then started to laugh, and I remembered Chotay Dada was outside, observing this encounter, probably thinking that I'd arranged this "secret" rendezvous because I was a boy-crazy Westernized wild child.

I turned and rushed out of the store, not daring to look back, figuring the boy was probably still laughing at me. Chotay Dada rose from the bench and followed, this time staying behind me. When we arrived at the Apple store, he walked up to a hipster store clerk who had a geometrical tattoo across his collarbone and a beard groomed to a defined point and said, in perfect English, "I would like to purchase an iPad."

As Chotay Dada discovered the wonders of iPads, I watched the corridor to see if the guy from Victoria's Secret might walk by. But the guy never appeared, and Chotay Dada completed his purchase. As we returned to the car he again remained a few feet behind. He'd obviously figured out I was ashamed, and though I did feel guilty, it wasn't enough to make me walk alongside him.

I played Radiohead as I drove home, the music accompanied by Chotay Dada's murmur as he moved through his prayer beads. He had the same nose as my father, big and studded with blackheads.

The song "Karma Police" started to play, the opening piano

rife with an angst that became increasingly urgent, a perfect song for a day like today. I turned it up cautiously, concerned Chotay Dada might find the music disturbing, but he didn't react, only kept on praying. As the drums kicked in and Thom Yorke began to sing, I finally figured out what Chotay Dada was murmuring. *La illaha il Allah.* There is no God but God.

Karma police

La illaha il Allah

Arrest this man he talks in maths

La illaha il Allah

When I pulled into the driveway, Chotay Dada said, "Thank you," with a sincerity that weighed heavily upon my already guilty conscience.

"You're welcome," I said.

"Coming?" he asked.

"After this song," I said in Urdu.

He walked toward the house, white Apple bag in one hand, prayer beads in the other, and then it was the best part, when the piano and guitar and drums came together and Thom Yorke's voice became so impassioned, so electric, that it reverberated inside and all around me, making me want to dance and weep at the same time, the part when Farah and I would toss our heads and drum our palms against the dash and sing about losing ourselves.

Though if either of us was lost, it was me. I wasn't proud of not sticking up for Farah, or kissing Ryan, or even walking a few feet in front of Chotay Dada, but I figured I'd leave my past behind and reinvent myself when I got to UPenn, into someone more fearless and confident and cool, who would make new friends with sweat-free ease.

I had a simple plan. Get through the summer. Get to Penn. Begin anew. Don't look back.

Three

MR. BLAKE TAUGHT AP World History and was my favorite teacher at Lincoln Prep. He was probably in his forties but dressed like a hipster, in skinny pants and formfitting blazers and Converse with rainbow laces. He'd been teaching for ten years but never acted jaded or bored, and he always managed to hold our attention, even first period Monday morning.

That Monday he began in his usual starting position, on the edge of his desk, ankles crossed, feet swinging.

"I know it's our last day of class and we're behind," he said, "but we barely touched on the Partition of India, which was one of the bloodiest events in the twentieth century. Not only that, but, as you learned from your reading, it was the largest mass migration in history."

He paused, then repeated "The *largest* mass migration in *history*" in his deep, radio-announcer voice that lent everything he said, even *hello*, a sense of gravitas. "This migration was an incredible upheaval for all those involved, and resulted in massacres and other tragedies. So, before we move on, I thought I'd ask if anyone in class knows any stories about Partition?"

This was one of Mr. Blake's favorite teaching methods, personalizing history. When we studied the Holocaust, he asked the Jewish kids to share family stories. But there were only two people in class who might have personal narratives about Partition, me and JJ, whose real name is Vijay. His freshman nickname had been "Va-jay-jay!," which was shortened to JJ after he proved his manhood by scoring a series of goals in some important soccer game.

Mr. Blake tried JJ first. "Mr. Karimple?"

JJ looked up with a startled "Yeah?"

"Would you mind me asking if anyone in your family was affected by Partition?"

He shrugged. "I don't think so. My family's from Kerala, that's like in the south, and as far as I know we didn't have to go anywhere during Partition."

"Oh, I see," Mr. Blake said, a little disappointed, though one hope remained. "Ms. Qureshi, what about you? Did Partition affect your family?"

"Yes," I said, which won me the attention of the entire class.

"Go on," Mr. Blake encouraged, leaning forward and

steepling his fingers underneath his chin.

"Uh . . ." I didn't talk much in class, and I didn't know any family stories. People didn't talk about Partition, or if they did, it was usually in general terms. Though my mother had said something happened to Chotay Dada, I didn't know what. But I really didn't want to disappoint Mr. Blake, whose comments at the end of my papers were always thoughtful and encouraging, who'd written college recommendation letters for me.

"Something pretty terrible did happen to my great-uncle," I said.

"Would you mind telling us?" Mr. Blake asked gently. "You don't have to, of course."

Given that half the class was already nodding at me empathetically, in anticipation of the tragedy to come, I felt even more of an obligation to deliver. I recalled what I'd read about Partition in my textbook, and the few things I'd heard mentioned. Train massacres, women jumping into wells rather than be raped.

Once I started, I couldn't stop.

"I call my great-uncle Chotay Dada," I said. "When Partition happened, his parents left to go from India to Pakistan, but Chotay Dada stayed a little longer, because . . . because he was in love with this girl. She was Hindu, and he was Muslim, so they had to keep their love secret, because her family wouldn't approve, but he couldn't leave India without saying goodbye to her and telling her he'd always love her, no matter what."

Next to me, one of Ian's rings flashed as he clasped his hand to his chest. It was a Bollywood version of Partition, but it was working.

Emboldened, I continued. "But when Chotay Dada got to the girl's house, her father threatened to kill him if he took one more step. Before Chotay Dada could even say anything in his defense, the girl's brothers came out of the house and started chasing him with knives, and Chotay Dada barely escaped with his life.

"He realized there was no way he could say goodbye to the girl, so he got on the next train to Pakistan. As it was about to leave the station, a Hindu mob attacked the train. They started to kill everyone—men, women, children . . ."

Someone gasped. Ian looked stricken.

For the first time in my life, I had control of the room.

"A few men from the mob went through Chotay Dada's car, slaughtering people. Chotay Dada ducked down, and somehow they missed him. But Chotay Dada knew it wasn't over yet, so he smeared himself with someone else's blood and lay down in between two dead bodies. The mob went back through the train, searching for any survivors. He knew if he moved even an inch they'd kill him, so as they went past he lay as still as he could, and prayed he'd see his love again. . . ." I paused, both impressed and taken aback by my penchant for melodrama.

The class was leaning toward me now, like my words were magnetic.

"The mob finally got off the train, and the train finally left for

Pakistan, but it was hours before Chotay Dada dared to move. When he walked through the train, all he saw were corpses. He was the only one left alive."

"Wow," Ian said.

Mr. Blake, who'd been listening with a bowed head, put on his wire-rimmed glasses and resumed control. "Thank you for sharing, Ms. Qureshi," he said. "Let us all learn from the story Ms. Qureshi so generously shared with us."

As the class's attention shifted to the front of the room, I realized I was exhausted.

"One million people died during Partition—Muslims and Hindus and Sikhs—and each one of them has a story," Mr. Blake continued. "Imagine your family's lived in a town for generations, and then one day you're told, sorry, you're no longer welcome here. We talk about the birth, death, and division of nations, but we so often forget the human toll behind political maneuvers. We still forget them. It's stories like these that remind us that every action has a consequence, and that it's most often those without a say who suffer the most."

We moved on in history class, but my story refused to die. Up until then, the topics of the day had been who did what during Natasha's game and whose boobs were in a photo uploaded to #10minutesinheaven. It was my last day of class at Lincoln Prep, but instead of feeling suddenly nostalgic for a high school I'd complained about since I'd enrolled, I spent it hoping Ryan wouldn't tell people about our crappy kiss. Thankfully, the topic of Ryan and me didn't start trending. Unfortunately, my Partition story did.

Right before lunch, a freshman I'd never seen before stopped me and said, "Hey, man, sorry about your uncle getting gassed."

"No one got gassed during Partition," I told him. "You're thinking of a different genocide."

When Sarah Martin asked me outside the cafeteria if it was true my grandmother gave birth to my father in a train full of dead people, I decided to skip lunch. Our newly remodeled library had a nook on the second floor, a quiet corner all the way at the end of the stacks that was flooded with sunlight in mid-afternoon. Farah and I used to hang out there sometimes, leaning against the floor-to-ceiling windows and talking and reading and illegally snacking, basking in the warmth of the sun and each other's company.

I hadn't been here in a while, and when I arrived I found Farah already there, drawing in her notebook. Her drawings were amazing, though she was never happy with them. She'd recently become more experimental with her headscarf; today she'd wrapped it like a turban, except the turban was lopsided. I wondered if I should tell her, or if she intended it that way. With Farah you never knew.

"Jelly Belly?" she asked, gesturing at the bag of jelly beans tucked between her thighs. Candy was Farah's comfort food, which meant her parents were probably at it again. They fought a lot, usually about money.

"No, thanks."

If we were still close, I would have asked her if her parents had fought, would have told her about Chotay Dada's visit and the guy from Victoria's Secret, described his green/bronze/brown eyes and his scar. Given our current circumstances, I figured I should probably leave her alone, except I still missed her like crazy, and it had already been such a long day. So I sat down next to her, picked up the bag, and searched for my favorite flavors, banana and very cherry.

"So, our last day of class ever," I said.

She ignored my attempt at conversation and kept drawing intently. A train, a face in each window, some bleeding, some screaming, some wild.

"You heard my story!" I exclaimed.

"I think even Principal Stone has heard it by now. How come you never told me this tragic tale?" she said, adding a sinister curl to one passenger's mustache.

"You never asked."

She tapped her teeth with the edge of her pen. "It's not true, is it?"

I shook my head.

"That's a pretty fucked-up thing to lie about."

"I know, but Mr. Blake asked for Partition stories, and he's been so supportive. I probably got into Penn because of the rec he wrote me. I didn't want to disappoint him."

"Yeah," Farah conceded. She closed her notebook. Its entire

cover was filled with drawings—a dragon playing guitar, scrolling vines and arabesques. "I heard you had to spend ten minutes with Ryan."

"Yeah."

Farah pulled up her sleeve, started outlining her veins in purple ink. "So what did you do?"

"We talked."

"About what?"

I knew if I told her the "hair makes a woman" comment, she'd go berserk, so I opted for a lesser evil. "He told me he dated a Sri Lankan girl whose hair smelled like coconuts."

"You're kidding." She tucked a stray strand back underneath her headscarf and looked at me with her intense, kohl-rimmed eyes, done up like Amy Winehouse's. Farah made her own kohl, with castor oil and ghee.

"Did he try to hook up with you?" she asked.

Lying to my history class—not so difficult. Lying to Farah—really f'ing hard.

"No," I said.

"Really, because I heard you gave him a blow job."

"What?" I shrieked, horrified. "Sick! Who told you that?"

"I made it up."

"Why? To test me?"

She shrugged.

"What, you don't trust me?" I replied, indignant.

"Relax, I believe you. What else did you talk about? I don't suppose you told him he's an unkind, overprivileged bully and bigot?"

"I didn't tell him off," I admitted. "But having to spend ten minutes with him left a bad taste in my mouth."

Literally.

Farah furrowed her brow, incredulous. "Did you think it wouldn't? You know what a jerk he is. Or do you?"

"Of course I do."

"Then why did you laugh that day?"

"Why did you have to sit on that stupid couch?" I countered.

"Maybe I was tired of having to sit in the back of the bus," she said.

"So now you're the Muslim Rosa Parks? Why does everything have to be political with you? Just because you wear hijab doesn't mean you have to stop being fun."

She sighed. "I don't want to talk about this right now."

Farah could be so self-righteous sometimes, thinking she was better than everyone else. "I'm late for something," I told her.

"I guess you better go then," she said, her voice stiff.

I gritted my teeth and went hunting for someplace I could be alone.

Four

THE MAIN DRAG OF my hometown of Clover Creek was called High Street, several blocks of cute boutiques and restaurants, an Irish pub, a fancy barber, an organic ice cream parlor. This quaint commercial district bordered Clover Creek's town park, which featured more than fifty acres of grassy fields, leafy woods, babbling brooks, tennis courts, playgrounds, an arched stone bridge, a band shell, and a rose garden. It was the kind of town where crime consisted of bored teenagers knocking down mailboxes, and the residents were generally overeducated and socially conscious, the kind of people who put wheatgrass in their smoothies, campaigned vigorously to keep Walmart out, drove hybrid SUVs, made their kids play soccer and learn Chinese.

The Clover Creek farmers' market took place Wednesdays and Sundays in the park's eastern parking lot, rows of tables displaying the rich and varied hues of earth's bounty: crisp green heads of lettuce and bloodred beets, jars of golden honey and pink strawberry preserves, goat's milk soaps and homemade hummus. My mother had sent me here to buy blackberries for my father. He'd never eaten one before he came to America but it was love at first bite. Personally, I found both the strawberry and blueberry to be superior, but there was no accounting for taste. I stopped to sample chia seed pita chips and all four flavors of hummus, and listened to the proprietor Sophie, who, guessing her audience, told me how the hummus had been made from sustainable, fair trade olive oil from small villages in Palestine. I bought the lemony garlic, seven dollars for a small tub, figuring when my mother complained I'd tell her I'd done it to help the Muslims.

I was on my way to Crowler's Berry Stand, picking at a chia seed stuck between my teeth, when I saw the guy from Victoria's Secret. He was at the berry stand, holding a straw bag, its handle decorated with ribbons and seashell strings. A moment later, an elderly woman wearing a hip outfit of black capri leather pants and an embroidered white kaftan-style shirt appeared next to him. One of the fruit stand employees, a bearded man in faded denim overalls, left his post to greet them.

Our encounter at Victoria's Secret had been up close, so now I took in the entirety of him: high-top green Converse, jeans rolled up past his ankles, a red plaid shirt with sleeves pushed up to his elbows, thick, tousled light brown surfer hair that swept across his forehead. I was too far away to see his eyes.

I wanted very much to see his eyes.

And it happened, like a scene in a rom-com. He turned his head and noticed me standing forty feet away. He immediately waved, and then said something to his elderly companion, who looked at me, too.

I had three choices: run away like a coward, stay still like a fool, or walk toward them like a normal person. My heart pounding, I took one step and then another, painfully conscious of how they were both watching me, wishing I'd put serum in my hair and concealer on my face.

The guy from Victoria's Secret bounded forward, closing the distance between us in a moment's leap.

"It's you," he declared. He seemed so happy to see me that I immediately smiled back, keeping my lips closed, in case there were still seeds in my teeth.

In the sun, his eyes were flecked with gold.

"I'm Jamie," he said.

"Shabnam."

As we shook hands, I could feel his scar beneath my fingers, smooth, slightly raised.

"What brings you here?" he asked. "I don't suppose it was me."

Did that count as flirting?

I swallowed, reminded myself to think before speaking. "I came to buy some blackberries for my dad. He loves blackberries."

"Blackberries? Let's see what Farmer C has got."

I followed him to the blackberry section. After surveying the fruit, he selected a pint from the center.

"Come," he said. "There's someone I want you to meet."

We walked over to the elderly woman, who had resumed her conversation with the man in overalls.

"Aunt Marianne," Jamie said.

She held her hand up, signaling for him to wait. She was wearing a badass turquoise and silver ring that spanned two fingers. After saying something I couldn't hear that made the farmer burst out laughing, she gave him a clap on the shoulder and turned around.

There was no confusion about the color of Aunt Marianne's eyes—an intense, cerulean blue. She had soft cheeks and wrinkles that extended, whisker-like, from the corners of her lips and eyes. Her hair was a shock of white, coiled at the top of her head in a bun held together by a red ballpoint pen.

"Aunt Marianne, this is the interesting scar girl," Jamie said. "Her name is Shabnam. We randomly ran into each other. What a coincidence, huh?"

Interesting scar girl. He'd obviously told her about our awkward encounter.

"Ah. Coincidence, indeed." Aunt Marianne's voice was husky,

and strong. She stuck her hands in her back pockets. "Nice to meet you," she said, though her tone indicated otherwise.

"Hello," I replied.

"Shabnam's here to buy blackberries for her father," Jamie informed her.

"Don't bother," Aunt Marianne said.

"Sorry?" I said, trying not to be intimidated by her brusqueness. Maybe she was only nice to farmers.

She took the pint of blackberries from Jamie and held them to my face. "Look. Smell."

I looked, and I smelled. "I can't really smell much."

"Because it's too early," she explained. "They're not dark enough, and they don't have the soul of summer yet. You know, *blackberry, blackberry, blackberry.*"

I had no idea what she was talking about. "It's okay, my dad won't be able to tell," I said.

Aunt Marianne made a hmmfff noise, which I assumed was in judgment of my father.

"Aunt Marianne's a fruit Nazi," Jamie said.

"I'm *discriminating*," she corrected him.

Jamie laughed and kissed her on the cheek, which caused her lips to turn up, a little.

"Jamie," she said, "we gotta move."

"One sec," he said. "It's not every day I get to buy blackberries for a beautiful girl."

I swear I almost looked around to see who he was talking about.

But it was me he was calling beautiful.

"Hey," Jamie said to her, "didn't your pie girl just cancel on you? Shabnam, do you happen to be looking for a summer job?"

I'd graduated last week and the rest of the summer remained uncertain. I'd been considering getting a job at the mall, but I did not want to work for this woman, who was currently frowning at me.

"Aunt Marianne owns Andromeda's Pie Shack, the pie stand in the park?" Jamie continued.

"I know it." I'd never had pie from there, but I'd heard people rave about it.

"As pie girl," Jaime continued, "all you have to do is open up the shack Monday through Friday at four p.m., and you're done when the pies sell out for the day. But you have to get there at three thirty; that's when I deliver the pies. And the shack's only open for a month, so it's not a huge time commitment."

If Jamie delivered the pies that meant if I took this job I'd see him almost every day. For a whole month.

"She'd be perfect, don't you think?" Jamie remarked to his aunt. "Please?"

Aunt Marianne's frown deepened, her nostrils flaring as she exhaled sharply, so I was surprised when I heard her say, "You haven't told her how much it pays."

"Twenty-five dollars a day, even if the pies sell out in half an hour, which they sometimes do," Jamie said. "That cool?"

"Yeah . . . if that's cool with everyone else," I said.

"All right!" Jamie exclaimed, giving me a high five, which

of course I almost missed. "Why don't you meet me at the shack at three thirty p.m., the first Monday in July. You know where it is?"

"Yes," I said. "First Monday in July. I'll be there."

I said goodbye to them, Jamie's excited grin a marked contrast to Aunt Marianne's grim expression.

When I reached home, I realized I had no blackberries, because Jamie hadn't bought them, and neither had I. But what did it matter, when in the very near future I would have a summer job, and Jamie all to myself, almost every day.

Five

ANDROMEDA'S PIE SHACK WAS tucked away in a corner of the park, along a paved pathway that bisected a field of dandelion and clover. It was a small wooden shack with a tin roof and a large checkout window. A portrait of Andromeda took up one whole side. She had a long face, small lips, dark eyes, and tumbling curls. Her face was fading, but someone had recently reinvigorated her hair with gold shimmery spray paint.

"Won't you be hot in there?" my mother asked dubiously.

I would be, but not in the way she imagined.

We were on a rare family outing. My mother wanted to see my future place of work, and had forced my father to come along. Rivulets of sweat ran down his head, weaving through his ring of hair. It amazed me that despite his eating habits and lack of exercise, he was mostly skinny—with thin limbs, narrow shoulders, and a concave chest—except for his gut, which was so large you wondered how his toothpick legs could support it.

"We are within walking distance to donuts," my father said.

"When I tell you to go for a walk, you refuse, but you'll walk for donuts?" my mother said.

"I'd prefer to drive but we left our car at home," my father answered. "Anyway, I am going."

"Dad, if we let you go alone you'll probably get lost walking home," I said.

"Nonsense," he said.

"What nonsense?" my mother exclaimed. "You get lost in your own house."

"I could have a donut," I said.

My mother made a noise of protest, but it was mostly for show, because she loved the donuts, too.

The town of Clover Creek may have had a cutesy High Street and a lovely park, but the donut shop was its crowning glory. Ye Olde Donut Shoppe used to have blah donuts and bland coffee, and an extremely grouchy and increasingly senile old man behind the register, who'd give you the wrong change and then yell at you for saying he did. Still, it was a town institution, so everyone felt a loss when it suddenly closed the summer before my junior year. For months it lay dark and abandoned, until one night someone even stole the white Ye Olde Donut Shoppe letters, a crime that made the front page of the *Clover Creek Crier.*

Then one day, construction began. When it reopened, it retained its cute Tudor exterior, like a cottage in a Disney Shakespeare village, but instead of bad lighting and a dirt-colored linoleum floor the interior was sleek and modern with a Moroccan flair. The floor was now a warm wood, and next to the glass display case was a long, gray slab counter with red bar stools. The opposite side was lined with wooden tables and red-cushioned benches. Every other window was covered with embroidered red carpet, and over each table hung a ceiling lantern of carved brass and multicolored glass. In the back was a cherry-red CD jukebox, and between the jukebox and the arched hallway that led to the bathroom was a floor-to-ceiling custom-built bookshelf, with a step stool and a sign that said "Ye Olde Book Exchange." If you looked hard enough, you might uncover a treasure. I'd once found a leather-bound *The Complete Works of Jane Austen*, and Farah had discovered one of her favorite books, *The Unbearable Lightness of Being* by Milan Kundera.

And my God, the donuts. The dough light and airy, gently dusted with sugar, and filled with delicious things like chocolate cream, fresh fruit preserves, custard, and my favorite, Nutella. Rapture at first bite.

I immediately brought Farah, and it became our hangout. We had our own favorite table, two down from the old Bosnian men who came almost every day to drink coffee and play cards. We soon became friends with the owner, Dino. He was like the uncle you always wished you had, handsome and dignified, even in his tracksuit, with a twinkle in his eyes and a kind word for everyone. He let me put eight Radiohead CDs in the jukebox. I played Radiohead whenever I was there, to the point where Dino once requested the unplugged version of "Creep."

"Hello!" Dino exclaimed when I walked in with my parents. "Mr. Qureshi and the Qureshi sisters!"

"Oh," my mother demurred.

"Which one is the younger sister?" I challenged him.

"Shabnam," my mother reprimanded, blushing.

"Where is lemon custard?" my father demanded.

"Sorry, but they're sold out. A lot of customers were in the mood for lemon this morning," Dino told him.

As my mother and Dino chatted and my father figured out what he wanted, I scored my favorite table. The card players weren't there today, their table occupied by an Asian woman with adorable twins, moving seamlessly in and out of a language I guessed was Korean as she talked to them. I wished I could do that with Urdu. Farah could burst into it at will, but when I spoke I had to think first, proceed with caution.

"I'm going to put a song on the jukebox," I told my parents.

"Don't you get sick of listening to this band?" my mother asked. She wasn't that into music and couldn't understand how it could affect my mood, my emotions. In the car, she turned the volume low, so it wouldn't distract whoever was driving and we could hear each other talking. Except that was part of the point, to stop talking, to let your mind go, to feel.

Though once in a while, she'd sing along with some old Bollywood song and rock her head a little and you knew she felt it, too.

"I do listen to other bands," I said, "but I will never get sick of Radiohead. It's not like all their songs are the same; in fact, it's the exact opposite."

My father had already gobbled down his donut, and was eyeing my mother's.

"Eh?" my mother said, moving it toward her. "You think I can't see you?"

My father frowned. He looked over, debating whether it was worth getting up and standing in line. Laziness prevailed, and then Dino miraculously appeared with another. "Since we didn't have lemon, try this new flavor—blackberry jam."

My dad looked like his head might explode at this merger of his favorite dessert and favorite fruit.

"Any funny stories today, Dino?" I asked.

Dino scratched his salt-and-pepper chin. "Not today, ah, but yesterday. This lady comes to the shop, smart, educated, expensive handbag type. She asked me where I was from, I said Bosnia. She said, 'Bosnia? I didn't know Bosnia had pastries. How interesting. Is it very advanced?' We had Olympics in Sarajevo in 1984, but I could tell she was imagining only shepherds. And name me a country with no pastries!"

"Papua New Guinea," my father said.

"It was a rhetorical question," I said.

"No, it wasn't," my father objected.

"Irfan, let him finish," my mother admonished.

"The end of the story is that she ate one donut and then ordered a dozen," Dino said.

"Of course she did," my mother said.

After Dino politely excused himself, my mother declared, "Such a nice man," before returning to the condition of the pie shack. "Are you sure you want to work there? How about something in the mall, where it's air-conditioned? I worked in the mall the summer after high school, at Merry-Go-Round."

"What's that?" I asked.

"Cheap, trendy fashion," she replied. "You know, all the latest fads."

My mother moved to the US when she was seventeen and did her last year of high school on Long Island, which was why she thought she understood what it was like to grow up here, except our experiences and attitudes couldn't be more different. She actually had two boys ask her to senior prom, and politely refused, because her faith forbade it, while I couldn't even imagine having two different guys ask me out, much less saying no to both.

"I'll be fine at the shack, trust me," I said.

"*Wah!* Phenomenal donut," my father exclaimed, looking down at his last remaining bite as he licked jam from his fingers.

"Hey, speaking of blackberry, have you ever read the poem 'Meditation at Lagunitas' by Robert Hass?" I asked him. I'd

Googled "blackberry blackberry blackberry" after meeting Aunt Marianne and found out it was a phrase from this poem.

"I have not had the pleasure of reading it, if it is indeed a pleasure," my father replied. "I often find Western poetry lacking in heart."

"That's ironic," I said. It went past my father, but my mother shot me a *be nice* warning look. "I liked it but I don't think I really got it. I printed it out; I can give it to you if you want."

"Of course," my father replied. "Who could say no to a poem?"

Six

THE FIRST DAY OF work, I arrived early, sitting down on a bench across from the shack. I'd brought *Midnight's Children*, another one of Farah's favorite books, to read, but I was too nervous to focus. After rereading the first paragraph several times, I gave up. A couple in a sundress and tuxedo walked by hand in hand, followed by a photographer. Lots of couples had engagement and wedding photos taken in the park, especially on the stone bridge.

"Pause," the photographer called out. She was really petite, with a huge camera. "Now turn your head toward one another, and look back at me. Good. Smile!"

The couple smiled broadly. They were young and cute and happy. When they first met, they'd probably known nothing about each other, and now here they were, secure enough in their relationship to hire a professional photographer to commemorate it. How did you get from there to here? I'd never even been on a date.

"Greetings."

I'd been so caught up in the couple I hadn't noticed Jamie approaching from the other side of the hill.

"And a good day to you, Mrs. Joan Milton," he added.

One thing that made me feel a little less nervous about Jamie, aside from his overt friendliness, was that he sometimes said weird stuff, too.

"Who?" I asked.

He gestured at the bronze plaque nailed to the bench. "In memory of Mrs. Joan Milton, devoted wife and mother, 1924–1973," he read.

"Oh. I didn't even notice," I confessed.

He sat down on the bench, ankle on knee. Both his Converse were duct taped at the toe. He slowly drummed his fingers against his thigh, his foot shaking at a much faster rhythm. It impressed me that he could fidget at two speeds at once.

Jamie pulled out a silver pocket watch, flicking open its engraved lid with his thumb. "We've got a little time," he said.

"Nice watch," I said.

"Thanks. It was my grandfather's. I never met him, but this was his prized possession." He draped his arm along the bench, the pocket watch dangling from his hand. His jeans were rolled up again, and I noticed how his light brown leg hair started in a neat, even line above the ankle. Nothing about my body hair was that civilized.

"I never got to know either of my grandfathers," I said.

"Where are you from?" Jamie asked.

"My parents are from Pakistan," I said.

"Ever been to K2?"

"No. Never been to Pakistan and anyway, I don't like heights."

"It's easy when you're climbing something. Don't look down, or even too far ahead. Focus on where you are in that moment."

"Well, if I ever decide to climb the world's second highest mountain, I'll keep that in mind," I said.

As Jamie laughed, he tossed his head, his sun-kissed hair flying off his forehead. Only a few minutes in and I'd already made him laugh. Yes!

"Are you going to go one day? Pakistan, I mean, not K2," he clarified.

"I doubt it. My dad's parents are dead, and my mom's parents lived here before they died, and I only have distant relatives left in Pakistan. And a few in India, apparently, who didn't migrate in 1947."

"What happened in 1947?"

"The British partitioned India into India and Pakistan. Well, into what was then East and West Pakistan, but anyway. It was the largest mass migration in history. Fifteen million people displaced, one million killed." As I said this, my voice became a little deeper, more inflected, an unconscious imitation of Mr. Blake.

"Killed by whom?" he said.

"It's complicated, but it was kind of everyone killing each other."

"Cool. I mean, not cool, obviously," he said, blushing a little. "But your family was okay?"

"Well . . ." The aftermath of the Chotay Dada story had made me uneasy, like I'd violated his privacy, even though no one who'd heard it had any idea who he was. I'd never imagined I'd tell it again, but I saw how Jamie had turned to face me, one leg up on the bench, his duct-taped toe almost touching my thigh; eyes, body rapt by my promise of a story.

I remembered something Mr. Blake had said once in history class—*to paraphrase Frank Herbert, whoever controls the story controls the universe.*

How could I deny him now? How could I deny this guy anything?

"Well, my great-uncle, I call him Chotay Dada, he lived in Delhi, and Hindus and Sikhs were coming from what is now Pakistan, and the Muslims were fleeing to Pakistan, because if they stayed they'd be murdered, and Chotay Dada's whole family left, but he refused to go with them, because he was in love with this Hindu girl."

I told him how the girl's family threatened to kill Chotay

Dada, about the attack on the train.

"Man, he must have had some serious survivor's guilt," Jamie noted.

I hadn't thought of that.

"So what happened to the girl?"

"What girl?" I said.

"The girl that Chotay Dada loved. Did they ever get together?"

I'd never considered the fate of their romance. "She . . . she figured out he was on the train, and when she heard everyone on the train died, and that her own brother was part of the mob, she killed herself by jumping into a well."

"Into a well?" Jamie repeated.

"Yes. She was devastated, and . . . pregnant."

"Man." Jamie touched my shoulder for a brief, wondrous moment, and I thought I'd kill a whole village if it made him touch me again.

"Did Chotay Dada know she was pregnant?" he asked.

"Uh, no . . . not at the time. But before she died, she wrote a letter to him, telling him she was."

"Oh. But you said she thought he was dead," Jamie said.

He was a good listener, and my lie was becoming too tangled. "She wrote the letter before she heard he was dead, and gave it to someone who was going to Pakistan so they could deliver it to him. And he did get it, eventually, but by the time he got it, she was already gone."

Jamie exhaled, running his scarred hand through his hair. "That's some story."

"It's only one story of a million," I said solemnly.

"Fascinating," he declared.

Shabnam Qureshi, Partition Ambassador to White People.

"Why are you smiling?"

I covered my mouth, embarrassed. "Nothing."

Jamie checked his pocket watch. "We should move."

I followed him down the path to the small parking lot, where Jamie slapped the hood of a black, boxy Dodge minivan, a flashy red stripe down its middle.

"Thirty-one years, 185,000 miles," he said. "She may look old, but she's forever young."

"Wow," I said, as if I knew anything about cars.

In the back of the van were lots of bamboo steamer baskets. He handed me a stack, and we took the shortcut to the shack. Jamie bounded up the grassy hill, waiting for me at the shack's side door. On the way down, I took careful steps and he flew, arms spread wide. When I arrived at the minivan, he was holding two dandelions.

"I got you a wish," he said.

I wished for Jamie to like me, and blew. Jamie demolished his with one powerful breath, but in spite of my best effort, a few stubborn seeds still clung to mine.

"Airplane!" Jamie cried.

As I looked up, he yanked off the remaining seeds.

I smiled. "Isn't that cheating?"

"The rules of dandelion blowing are made to be broken," he informed me solemnly. I giggled, though I wasn't sure if he was being funny or serious, but then he winked. "Let's keep moving."

By the time we'd brought up all the pies, I was sweating. Jamie and I opened all the baskets and lined the pies on the display case shelves, their crusts so elegantly braided and lattice tops so perfectly woven they could have graced the cover of a gourmet food magazine.

"Smells good in here now, doesn't it?" Jamie said. "This is my smell of summer."

"Do you do this every summer?"

"Usually I come for a few weeks before, help Aunt Marianne get going. But the woman who helps her bake has bad gout, so I offered to stay till the shack closes."

One month. Four weeks. In Bollywood films love blossomed in the course of a single song—a chase, a dance, a kiss. Surely, by that perspective, four weeks would be long enough for a kiss.

"You've got that secret smile on your face again," Jamie said. "What are you thinking?"

"Sorry," I replied, embarrassed, but also pleased that he was paying so much attention.

"Don't be. You're beautiful when you smile."

Of course, this made me smile more.

He was the first boy to call me beautiful, and now he'd done it twice. You wouldn't repeat a compliment if you didn't think it was true.

As I squatted next to Jamie in front of the display case, I tilted my head in an attempt to get a discreet whiff of my pits. Definitely not beautiful. I pressed my arms into my sides.

"So, in case you can't tell what kind of pie it is, each one has a sticker on the pan. These are *b*, for blueberry. These are *p*, for pecan, not her famous chocolate pecan, which would be *cp*. These are *sr*, strawberry rhubarb. What else . . . every day you should write the kinds of pies on this big pad here, prop the pad up on the stand, and sell 'em till they're gone. You can leave the proceeds in the money box, me or Aunt Marianne will collect it later. When the pies sell out, clean up, lock up, and you're done."

He turned in a circle as he surveyed the shack, tapping his thigh, bopping his head to some internal beat. The shack's interior was spartan: a small folding table, a metal money box, a metal stool splattered with white paint, a large, white drawing pad leaning against a stand, a stack of foldable pie boxes tied loosely with twine.

"Yeah, I think that's about it. Do you have any questions for me?"

"Uh . . ." I grasped at one, not wanting him to leave. "Why is it called Andromeda's?"

"She had a happy ending."

"What?" I said, wishing I had Googled her before.

"With Perseus. Well, being chained naked to the rocks was a

bummer, but after that things went pretty well. Also, it was the name of Aunt Marianne's favorite cat. She was pure white with a real grumpy face."

"The cat or Aunt Marianne?" I blurted, immediately regretting it. How could I crack a joke about his family on the first day?

Thankfully Jamie laughed. "Aunt Marianne's a sweetheart. It can take her a while to warm up, that's all." He hopped onto the stool, hooking his Converse underneath the metal bar. "Hey, did you bring some music? I have an old iPod and speakers in the car. You want them?"

"Sure."

He returned a moment later, still not sweaty but definitely out of breath. After setting up the music, he stretched his arms above his head and cracked his knuckles loudly. When Farah did this, it drove me crazy, but with Jamie, I found it kind of sexy.

"Shabnam—what does it mean?" he said.

"It means morning dew," I said.

"Morning dew. I like that." He picked up the garbage bag full of empty bamboo baskets, tossing it over his shoulder like Santa Claus. "Well, Morning Dew, I'm off. I'll see you tomorrow. Call Aunt Marianne if you need anything."

It was 4:01 p.m., and when I lifted the shutter all the way there were already three people waiting outside. The pies sold out by 5:15. The most cumbersome aspect was folding the box for the pie, but once I got the hang of it, it took only a few seconds. Pie seemed to make people stupidly happy. It was an easy job, and I would have done it for free, just to hang out with Jamie.

Tomorrow, though, I had to remember to wear extra strength antiperspirant.

Seven

I WOKE THE NEXT morning to a letter slipped underneath my door, three legal size pages, front and back, covered with my father's freakishly neat, perfectly proportional handwriting, the letters exactly even, the words evenly spaced.

Dear Shabnam,

Thank you for the poem. From what I understand, in his poem "Meditation at Lagunitas" Mr. Robert Hass is addressing Plato's claim that objects we can see and experience in this world, the world of bodies, as Ibn Arabi referred to it, are mere shadows of an ideal form that exists elsewhere. For example, the rose that you see in a garden, no matter how beautiful, is only an imperfect shadow of the Form of the rose, which exists beyond our reality, and is perfect and unchanging. Mr. Hass seems to be challenging both this Platonic notion and the concept that language is separate, and separates us, from the experience of an object, the notion that, as he writes, "a word is elegy to what it signifies." I believe he means that, to the contrary, we can experience objects, and concepts, and perfection, through language, that language is not detached from experience. At least this is my interpretation. I also appreciated his choice of blackberries. There have been times when I have eaten a blackberry and considered it perfection indeed.

One line from the poem was of particular interest—"Longing, we say, because desire is full / of endless distances." Longing and the distance of desire is a central theme in Urdu poetry as well. In this vein, as you have given me a poem, I thought I would return one. This poem is called "Kya Karen" by Faiz Ahmed Faiz, the great modern Urdu poet, and the translation is by me. It is one of my favorite poems by Faiz.

I have also attached some information to help you understand Urdu poetry, its basis in Islamic mysticism, etc.

Enjoy,
Dad

KYA KAREN (WHAT DO WE DO)—*Faiz Ahmed Faiz*

(translated by Irfan Qureshi)

The hundred thousand waits that
Are in your gaze and mine
The hundred thousand wounded hearts
In your body and mine
All the pens weakened by the absence
Of feeling in your fingers and mine
The unmarked graves of our footsteps
In every street
Of your city—and mine
The wounded, wounding stars
Of your night and mine
The roses of our mornings
That are torn and torn and torn again
All these wounds without a cure
All these tears undarnable
On some the ash of moonlight
On some the blood of dew
Tell me whether this even is
Is it real, or merely a web
Spun by the spider of my delusion—and yours
If it is, then what do we do
If it is not, still, what do we do
Tell me tell me
Tell me tell me

After reading the Faiz poem, I felt like crying. It was incredibly sad, and devastatingly beautiful. I hadn't asked my father for a detailed explanation of the blackberry poem, and couldn't believe he'd responded with a long letter about that and the traditions and tropes of Urdu poetry. Sure, it was poetry, but he'd still made an effort for me.

When I went downstairs, my father was on the couch, watching TV. His sabbatical had begun, which he apparently planned on spending in his study with the door closed, or on the couch in the den, eating fried *papad* and directing barbs at the boob tube.

As I poured myself cereal, I could hear the news filtering in from the den: strikes in Greece, civil war in Syria, a humanitarian crisis in Somalia. It made me think of a line from the Faiz poem: *the roses of our mornings / that are torn and torn and torn again*.

I joined him with my breakfast. "I really like the Faiz poem."

"Oh yes?" He looked genuinely pleased. Of course he was. Urdu poetry was his best friend. "Would you like to read more?"

I hadn't considered it, but now that I had a handwritten introduction to the genre, I might as well. "Sure."

A correspondent was reporting on the dire conditions in Syria. He stood in front of a pile of rubble that was once an apartment building, explosions in the background.

My father frowned. "Bloody Assad!" he said. "Bloody dictators!"

Commercial break. A dyed blonde in a poofy fuchsia dress and heels praised the ability of her dishwashing liquid to cut through grease. "No spots, and no need to rinse! Spend less time cleaning, and more time doing things you love—like eating salt and vinegar potato chips!" she exclaimed, hopping onto the kitchen table and digging into a bag of chips.

"Do we have any potato chips?" my father asked.

"No," I lied, knowing he'd be too lazy to go look.

He grunted and flipped to an Urdu news station, where there was a reporter standing in front of a pile of rubble that was once a Shia mosque in Pakistan.

"Bloody zealots!" my father said.

I glanced at my phone. Six hours until I saw Jamie.

This morning couldn't move fast enough.

Eight

THIS TIME WHEN JAMIE arrived, I was actually reading, trying to make sense of my father's dense Urdu poetry notes, which included diagrams, quotations from poems, rhyme schemes, and an introduction to Islamic mysticism.

"Greetings," Jamie said. "Your curls look nice."

My hand flew up to my hair. "Really?" I said, as if I hadn't spent half the morning washing my hair, applying a deep moisture treatment, plopping it with a microfiber towel I'd bought online, and using a diffuser.

"My first girlfriend had curly hair," he said. "Sixth grade. Dana Parker. She broke my heart. I've been a sucker for curls ever since. The darker, the better."

Dana Parker may have been a fool, but she had served me well.

Jamie sat down, draped his arm along the bench. I dared to lean back a little, imagining the slim margin of air between my body and his hand, an inch, maybe even less. An inch was nothing. An inch was an ocean.

The distance of desire.

He pointed at the pages in my lap. "That's some handwriting," he commented.

I loved how he noticed details, that he thought me and my possessions were worth paying such close attention to. It encouraged me to open up to him, but it also made me nervous, like what if after getting to know me, he decided I was no longer so interesting?

"What is it?" he asked.

"A letter my father wrote me."

"Where does he live?"

"What?" I said, and then laughed. "Oh, no, he lives with us. It's not a letter like that, it's more of a lesson."

"A lesson?" he said. "What about?"

"Urdu poetry."

"Urdu poetry," Jamie repeated. He took a Swiss Army knife out of his jeans pocket and an orange out of his shirt pocket, and started peeling the orange, cutting strips that went all the way around, falling into a neat pile on the bench.

"Will you teach me about it?" he asked, offering me an orange slice.

"About what?"

"Urdu poetry."

"What do you want to know?"

"What do you think I should know?"

"Umm . . ." I wasn't sure how to answer this, given that I was only learning myself, but I didn't want to disappoint Jamie. "I guess the first thing you need to know is a little about Sufism."

"Sufism?"

"Mystical Islam."

"Okay." Jamie popped the last orange slice in his mouth, tossed the peels into the garbage can a few feet away, wiped his palms on his jeans. "I'm all ears."

"All right. Well, the traditional form of Urdu poetry is called the ghazal, and it's inspired by the Sufis. The Sufis were, and are, I guess, Islamic mystics who saw themselves as lovers of God. They were literally mad with love for God—that's where the whole whirling dervish thing comes from, because some of them were so madly in love with Allah that they would dance in circles, for hours and hours, sometimes." I paused, realizing he might not understand the whirling dervish reference, but he nodded as though he did.

"The Sufis' ultimate goal is to destroy their ego, their materialistic desires, and become one with Allah. So they devote their whole lives to Him, praying, meditating, singing His praises, dancing, but of course they can really only become one with Allah when they die and go to heaven. A day a Sufi dies isn't called his death anniversary, it's called his wedding anniversary, because that's the day he's finally joined his beloved, as in God. I think that's pretty beautiful. I mean, a lot of the time you're taught to fear Allah, because on Judgment Day He might send you to hell, like He's a big, scary dude. But the Sufis, their relationship to Allah is centered around love. They worship Him because they love Him. To love is to worship, to worship is to love. They write poetry for Him, and dance and sing."

"Awesome," Jamie agreed. "Go on."

"So, Urdu poetry is inspired by Sufi poetry. All of Sufi poetry is about longing for the beloved, and you can't truly be with the beloved until you die, because your beloved is God. The Urdu ghazal is the same. The narrator is longing for the beloved he can never really have, at least not until he dies. Except you can read it on two levels, that the narrator's beloved is a human, or that it's Allah."

"So it's kind of metaphysical," Jamie said.

I wasn't quite sure what metaphysical meant, so I kept talking. "And, according to my father, the narrator of the poem is pretty much always male, but sometimes his beloved is a woman, and sometimes it's a handsome male youth. And time is basically divided into two types, the days and nights of separation, when the lover longs for the beloved, and the days and nights of union, when they come together, though this union never lasts long." I searched my father's notes. "The night of separation is painfully long, the day of union never long enough," I read. "However, without separation, what would become of the union? What is desire without distance? What is love without longing?"

"Your father wrote that?"

"Yes, which is weird because he's not like this in real life."

"Real life?"

"I mean, he sounds romantic here but he's not in real life, only in his poetic life."

"At least he's romantic in some life," Jamie said. "My stepfather's idea of romance is buying my mother a box of Russell Stover chocolates from CVS every Valentine's Day."

"At least he remembers Valentine's Day," I replied.

"Well, it's all really fascinating," Jamie declared. "I'd like to hear one of these ghazals."

"My father translated an Urdu poem for me; it's not a ghazal, but it's really good," I said. "I can bring it tomorrow."

"I'd love that, Morning Dew," he said, and checked his watch. "But now we gotta move."

Nine

THE NEXT DAY, AS I read Jamie the Faiz poem, he listened intently, eyes closed, head tilted back, only one foot in motion. When I read the lines, "*Tell me whether this even is / Is it real, or merely a web / Spun by the spider of my delusion*," my voice wavered a little, because this was the very question I had. I felt as though Jamie liked me, the way he looked at me, the way he listened, but until he said so, how could I know if it was real?

"*Tell me tell me*," I concluded.

After I finished, Jamie was silent for a minute. I watched his Adam's apple move with his breath. His neck was brushed with light golden stubble, and there was a small, claw-shaped scar in the space between his collarbones.

"*The hundred thousand waits that / are in your gaze and mine*," he recited suddenly. "Not a hundred, or a million, but a hundred thousand. I like it. A hundred thousand waits. A hundred thousand steps. A hundred thousand climbs."

He took such pleasure in the number that I didn't tell him "hundred thousand" was a common unit of counting in Urdu.

"A hundred thousand pies," I offered.

"That's a lot of pies," he said. "Is the ghazal a lot different from what you read?"

"I'm not sure," I confessed. "My dad hasn't given me one yet."

"Can I keep the poem?" he asked.

"Sure."

"Do you write poetry?" he said.

"Me? No."

"Do you speak Urdu?"

"Badly."

"And your father's name is Irfan Qureshi?"

"Irfan," I said, turning his short *a* into a long one. "But how do you know his name?"

"It says 'translated by Irfan Qureshi.'"

"Oh. Right."

"He must be pretty cool," Jamie said. "I'd like to meet him one day."

I must have looked incredulous, because he said, "What?"

"I doubt you're going to meet my parents. My mom would freak out that I was friends with a boy."

"And your dad?"

"My dad would talk your ear off about poetry but wouldn't even remember your name."

"What if I introduced myself like this?" He bowed, with a dramatic hand flourish. "Greetings, Mr. Qureshi. I am the hundredth thousandth Jamie. I am the lizard king, I am the maker of pies."

"Pie wallah," I said.

"What?"

"If you make or sell a particular thing, then you add wallah at the end. Biscuit wallah, newspaper wallah."

"So that means you're also a pie wallah," Jamie said.

"Yeah, I guess I am."

"The prettiest pie wallah in a hundred thousand miles," he pronounced.

I didn't know whether to thank him, or offer a return compliment, or a witty parry, so I stayed quiet, flushed and excited and wearing what was surely a stupidly happy smile.

Jamie checked his watch. "The pie wallahs need to move."

We were running late, so after we unloaded the pies—apple walnut, chocolate cream, and cherry bourbon—Jamie bowed again and left. I put on "Fake Empire" by The National, my favorite song from Jamie's most-played playlist. Like "Karma Police," it began with piano and built up to an awesome frenzy of piano and guitar and drums, but the best thing about it was the lead singer's voice—deep, sexy, alluring.

As I was about to lift the shutter, the door to the shack swung back open. Jamie was back.

"Hey, I love this song!" he exclaimed. "The pies can wait. Play it from the beginning and crank it up."

As the singer sang, "*Stay out super late tonight, picking apples, making pies*," Jamie and I looked at each other and laughed. Then he started to groove. There wasn't much room to maneuver, but he danced with ease, and I marveled at how confidently he navigated every space he encountered, narrow shack, big wide world, like it was all some playground for him to move through, fast and sure-footed. I felt inspired to do my own mini-groove, swaying my head and rocking a little, though I wished I could dance in front of someone with his same abandon. Even watching him made me feel happier, more free.

"*It's hard to keep track of you falling through the sky . . .*"

When the song ended, Jamie slapped his thigh and proclaimed, "Great song."

"Great song," I echoed.

Jamie raised the shutter all the way. There was a customer waiting outside, a fellow alumnus a few decades my senior, who'd finished an intense run, judging from the streaks of sweat on his gray Lincoln Prep T-shirt.

"Sorry about that," Jamie said to him. "Sometimes you just gotta dance."

Then he disappeared as suddenly as he'd returned.

Ten

I WAS IN LOVE with Jamie. He was my last thought before sleep, my first thought upon waking. He had conquered my heart, my mind. I danced to "Fake Empire" on repeat in my room. Stupid-happy smiles became my norm, even before 10:00 a.m., to the point where my mother jokingly asked me if I was on drugs.

I was aching to tell someone. Ian and Danny had left on their epic cross-country road trip, which, judging from their Instagrams, involved diners, drag queens, and lounging by hotel pools with frozen drinks. But even if they were here, it wouldn't have mattered, because the person I really wanted to tell was Farah. The silence between us was the sole dark cloud in these otherwise sunniest of times. But a little darkness was easy to ignore. I'd watched my mother do it for years. My khala, my mother's sister, had told me once that my mother had always wanted a big family, four kids. When I'd asked my mother if this was true, she said, "What does it matter? I have you. There are people in this world who can't have any children."

Last month, when my khala had come for my high school graduation, she told me my mother had had four miscarriages. My first thought when I heard this was I couldn't believe my parents had had sex five times.

My mother had only told me that the doctors said she couldn't get pregnant and then she did, with me. Her miracle baby. She'd never mentioned any miscarriages. Too unpleasant.

Outside, the lawn mower emitted a death groan. I glanced out my bedroom window. My father was struggling to cut the grass; when it came to work around the house, he was like an appendix; useless, a pain in the gut. Despairing, shoulders hunched, bits of grass pasted to his sweaty scalp, he labored to restart the mower, trudging behind it like condemned Sisyphus pushing the stone up the mountain.

I turned off "Fake Empire" and brought him lemonade.

He gulped it down so fast half of it spilled down his undershirt. "There are people who will do this for a small sum of money," he complained.

"Well, Mom's frugal, and you're on sabbatical," I said.

My father wiped his forehead with his undershirt, exposing

the whole of his pale, hairy belly. "You look like you're nine months pregnant," I said.

"Biologically impossible," he stated.

"I didn't mean it literally."

"Oh."

"I don't understand. How come you're an expert of figurative speech in Urdu poetry but can't understand it in real life?"

"Urdu poetry makes sense. Most conversation is idiotic."

"Is this conversation idiotic?" I demanded.

My father blinked. "Too early to say."

I'd lived with my father too long to take it personally. "Well, this might interest you—I'd like to read a ghazal."

Hearing one of his favorite words perked him up immediately. "Certainly," he said, abandoning the accursed mower. "But you should know that ghazals don't read like Western poems."

"What do you mean?"

"The ghazal is made up of two-line verses, and all of the verses share a meter and rhyme scheme. But they don't share, how do you say, a narrative. Thematically, each two-line verse is separate. Each verse can be read completely on its own."

"So why even put them together?"

"Because they share a meter and rhyme, something that is lost in translation. Reading Urdu ghazals in English will likely feel unsatisfactory. And you need to understand the tropes or it is hard to appreciate."

"Tropes?"

"Tropes. The most well-known is the rose and the nightingale."

"The rose and the nightingale?" I repeated.

My father cleaned the sweaty fog from his glasses with his lemonade-stained shirt and, exhausted from his mowing efforts, slowly lowered himself to the ground. Now that I was used to Jamie's lean fluidity, my father seemed even more plodding and out of shape, though he was weirdly flexible. Right now, he was sitting cross-legged with his feet resting on the opposite thighs, like a fat, grassy Buddha.

"The rose and the nightingale," my father said. "The rose is the symbol of perfect beauty, and the nightingale is in love with it. Even though the rose is cruel, and does not love him back, still the nightingale longs for the rose. It sings to the rose of its love. Each season, the rose blooms, it dies, and the nightingale mourns until a new rose, beautiful, cruel, takes its place."

"Sucks to be the nightingale," I muttered.

My father either didn't hear my comment or chose to ignore it.

"Would you like to hear a verse from a ghazal by the great Mirza Ghalib?" he offered.

"Yes, please."

My father recited the verse in Urdu. I only understood a few words, but then he translated it.

"*Sleep is his, pride is his, the nights are his / On whose shoulder your curls lay tangled*," he recited.

I shook my head. "I'm not sure I understand."

"In this verse, the narrator longs for his beloved but his rival is with her. While the narrator suffers, there is his rival, in high spirits, sleeping proudly next to the beloved, whose curls lay tangled across his shoulder. It is grammatically vague as to whether the beloved is a man or woman."

I hadn't expected my first verse from a ghazal to be sexy.

My mother's shadow fell between us. "What are you two doing?" she asked.

"Dad was telling me about ghazals," I said.

"Ghazals?" my mother repeated. "He can talk about ghazals after he mows the lawn."

"Later," I said to my father, and followed my mother inside.

She was reorganizing the drawers in the bottom of the large chestnut bookcase in the den. My mother was a full-time social worker for a domestic violence advocacy nonprofit, helping women obtain benefits and other services, but she also spent her weekends working: cooking, wiping, folding, sweeping, washing. She did things fathers normally do, like climb ladders to sweep away cobwebs near the roof of the house. She wasn't able to relax if she hadn't completed her mental to-do list for the day. But, even when on her knees scrubbing, my mother exuded an ethereal beauty, with her enormous, fawn-like eyes, creamy skin, and elegant neck, a Pakistani Audrey Hepburn. She worked the hardest of the three of us but still looked like she could feel a pea twenty mattresses below.

"You want some help?" I asked.

"You can sit and talk to me while I work," she suggested.

That's not what I meant, but I complied, opening a green binder of recipes my mother had torn from magazines. Fennel and honey rack of lamb, pomegranate chicken stew. I didn't think she'd actually made any of these dishes, probably because my father preferred Pakistani food.

"So, what is making you so happy these days?" she asked.

"Why does there have to be a reason?" I demanded.

"I don't know . . . it seems a sudden change, that's all."

"I'm happy because I'm done with high school, I like my job, I got into an Ivy League school. Life is good."

"And Farah?"

"What about her?" I said testily.

"She's your best friend, but she hasn't been over here in months. Her parents came to your graduation party but she didn't. Is everything okay between you?"

"It's fine. We've both been busy." I realized how ridiculous this sounded, considering I worked only a few hours a day.

"It has nothing to do with her wearing hijab?"

"No." Why did my mother never stop asking questions? At least if she'd had more kids, she would have had to divide her attention among us. "I gotta go do something."

I could tell my mother was upset, but not enough to almost cry. As I stood up, I rolled my eyes at the bookshelf. My mother used this bookshelf for decorative purposes; the only book on it was a copy of the Quran. The other shelves were filled with tchotchkes. My mother liked those ridiculous ceramic and porcelain figurines, the kind you get at Hallmark. She had dozens of them: owls and snowmen and sleds and ponies and kittens and a little cottage not unlike Ye Olde Donut Shoppe and even a giraffe on roller skates. When Farah first came to my house and saw them, she let out a yelp of glee. "I always wondered who bought this crap!" she said, and proceeded to make fun of them until she noticed I'd stopped laughing, at which point she slapped my shoulder lightly, said, "I only joke because I think they're so *awesome*," and moved on to another topic.

The highest shelf was reserved for my mother's Precious Moments angels, with their pale white skin, blonde or light brown hair, black teardrop eyes, and feathered wings. One was lying on a fluffy cloud, one was sitting on a silver bench and holding, I kid you not, a rose. They all had the same dopey look.

There were four in total.

Four angels. Four miscarriages.

There was no way. My mother couldn't be that cheesy.

Except she totally could. I wanted to barf, but it also made me sad, because my mother once imagined having four kids with a normal man and instead she ended up with my father and me. I frowned at the four lily-white, chaste, dumb-looking angels. I'd never be the daughter/confidante my mother hoped for, but I could be a little nicer.

"Let's go see a movie next week," I said, bending down and

kissing her smooth cheek.

She cupped my neck with her hand, pressing her warm face against mine. “My sweet girl,” she said.

If she only knew.

Eleven

JAMIE LOOKED SO CUTE in a baseball cap. He was wearing it backward, its band fixed with duct tape, his hair fanning out on either side. "How do you do, Morning Dew?" he asked.

This was his new greeting for me, just as the right side of Mrs. Joan Milton's bench had become his, the left mine. Only a week together and we already had traditions.

As he began to peel his orange, I said, "How do you know if an orange has the soul of summer?"

"Oranges are winter fruits. Season's over by May. But you will be happy to know the season of your favorite fruit is hitting its peak. They definitely have the soul of summer now. Blackberry pie is imminent."

"Great!" I said. I didn't bother telling him that I was no lover of blackberries, and anyway they now held more meaning to me than any other fruit, in both my real and poetic life.

"I learned a verse from a ghazal," I announced.

Jamie grinned. "I'm all ears, MD."

"*Sleep is his, pride is his, the nights are his / On whose shoulder your curls lay tangled*," I recited.

He was quiet, thinking it over, as he skillfully peeled the last of the orange. "What—" he began, but turned his head as if he'd heard something. A moment later, a young Asian kid on a skateboard started to coast down the hill.

Jamie jumped up. "Hey, man! Can I get a ride?"

The kid continued down the hill, coming to a slow stop in front of us. He balled his fists against his hips, one shoe scraping the ground, his peevish face sizing up Jamie. "You know how to ride?"

"Only done it a few times," Jamie said, "but loved every minute. What's your name?"

"Elliot."

"Nice to meet you, Elliot, I'm Jamie. I dig your board." As Jamie extended his hand with his trademark friendly grin, Elliot's annoyed scowl was replaced by a hesitant smile.

"How do I know you won't ride away with it?"

"I'll leave her as collateral," Jamie said, patting my shoulder.

Elliot looked at me doubtfully, and I bristled. He thinks I'm the prettiest pie wallah in a hundred thousand miles, I wanted to tell him.

"All right," Elliot said. "Just for a little bit, though, cuz I gotta get home."

"Five minutes," Jamie vowed. Elliot took Jamie's place on the bench and we watched as Jamie ran up the hill with the skateboard tucked under his arm like a surfer.

"Orange?" I offered.

Elliot made a face. "No thanks. Is he your boyfriend?"

"No."

"Do you like him?"

"Maybe."

"Why don't you tell him?"

I wiped the dribble of juice from my chin. "I'm scared," I confessed.

"Don't be a wuss diaper," Elliot said.

"Excuse me?"

"That's what my dad says about me being scared of the dark."

"Oh."

Jamie crested the hill with a loud whoop, bent low on the board. He raced past us, disappearing again.

"Wow," Elliot said. "Is he always that fast?"

"Yeah. But he's also a good listener," I said.

"How do you know if someone's a good listener?"

"Well, if they ask you questions. If they remember what you say."

"What if what you're saying is really boring? Does he listen then?"

I was spared further interrogation by the sight of Jamie speeding past us again. He flipped the board in midair and reversed course, taking his back foot off and losing his balance as he tried to slow down. When the board finally came to a stop, he jumped off and bowed.

I clapped, and Elliot said, with a mix of awe and confusion, "You can do an awesome 180 ollie but you suck at stopping."

"What can I say, Elliot? I'm a sucker for the rush," Jamie said. "Hey, Morning Dew, do you want to try?"

"Me? No way. I like to keep both my feet on the ground," I insisted.

"I could teach how you to stop some time," Elliott offered.

"That'd be great!" Jamie exclaimed as he handed the board back. "Let's definitely definitely do that."

As Elliot skated off, he looked back at Jamie twice, petulant kid turned earnest admirer. Jamie was too wired to notice or sit back down. He jumped onto the bench with one foot, switched legs, jumped off.

"How are you going to definitely definitely do it?" I asked.

"What?"

"How are you going to meet up with Elliot if he doesn't have your info?"

"With the kid?" He shrugged. "If we're supposed to hang out again, we will. I don't understand why people have to schedule everything. Why not see where life takes you?"

"Don't you ever plan?"

"Occasionally. For camping." He meant it as a joke, but I guessed it wasn't far from the truth. "You gotta do a little planning. If you want to leave the country, you have to buy a ticket. But when I leave the country, I won't have a guidebook, or a checklist, or Google where to go next."

"But what if you get lost?"

Good God. I sounded like my mother.

"That's the whole point, Morning Dew."

The adrenaline rush subsided enough for him to sit down again. "Those guys you see in Clover Creek, the suits walking to the train station in the morning, going to New York, working all day, walking back at night, getting up and doing it again, I could never do it, be some modern-day slave, shackled to an office all day, staring at a computer."

"Totally," I said, though I'd never thought about it much. Other than the fact that my major would be something in the humanities, English, maybe, I had no plan for my life, though when I imagined myself ten years from now it wasn't in a suit. "Speaking of shackles, what's the time?"

It was almost four by the time the pies were laid out in rows behind the glass: cherry, blueberry, the wildly popular chocolate pecan. Outside the half-closed shutter, the park resounded with the joyful titter of birds and the gleeful shrieks of children. Inside, only Jamie and me, standing close together in a narrow band of sunlight.

He peeled a curl from my sweaty forehead. "What was the verse? On his shoulder her curls lay tangled?"

As he inched closer, closer, I realized a kiss was imminent. I'd been dreaming about this moment, and now that it was here, I was—

"Morning Dew," Jamie said. "You're shaking."

Mortified, I hugged myself, trying to quiet my arms.

"Are you—"

Now it was the shutter that trembled, an insistent fist banging against metal. "Hello?" a voice called out. "Are you guys opening up? It's after four."

Jerk.

"Better not keep *him* waiting," Jamie said.

I'd sold the last pie when the clouds started rolling in, dark, menacing. The humidity rose, my hair with it. There was a rumble of thunder. Parents and nannies packed up their kids and started running. The clouds split open and the rain poured forth, clattering against the tin roof. The few people remaining dashed toward their cars or houses, shielding themselves with newspapers and purses. A gust of wind blew rain into the shack.

I hoped I hadn't freaked Jamie out. This was all so foreign to me. My best friend didn't date, my mother didn't approve of it. My only guy friends were Ian and Danny, two gay guys too scared to admit they liked each other. Right now my main discussion point on love was the doomed story of the nightingale and the rose.

It was raining too heavily to walk home. I had two options—sulk over being a hopeless wimp, or dance.

I put on Radiohead. When "Planet Telex" came on and Thom Yorke sang "*Everyone is, everything is broken*," I belted out the words, dancing like Farah sometimes did, head banging till it hurt.

From the corner of my eye, I thought I saw Jamie. I stopped, gasping for breath. As the spinning world fell back into place, Jamie was part of it, framed by the doorway, a gray wall of rain behind him.

First he'd witnessed my trembling nightingale act, and now my manic, furious dancing. The only way to make his impression of me any worse was to belch and fart simultaneously, something I'd witnessed my father do once.

"Please, don't stop dancing," he said.

I coiled my torrent of curly hair into a bun. "I must have looked ridiculous."

"You looked beautiful." He came closer, trailing water through the shack, and asked, "Will you dance with me?"

It was easy to do anything when it was preceded by *beautiful*.

"Okay," I said.

"You like Radiohead?"

"*Love* them."

"Then I'll pick a Radiohead song in your honor," he said, but first he took off his Converse and rolled up his jeans even higher.

"What are you doing?"

"We have to go outside. The shack's too small for a proper dance."

"But it's raining outside."

He grinned. "Exactly."

He set the speakers close to the door, turned the volume up all the way, and with a gasp I realized he'd chosen "Let Down," my absolute favorite Radiohead song. A sign from fate, if there ever was one.

He offered me his hand, and I accepted, and we stepped into the rain to the song's opening strains, electric with promise.

The rain had thinned to a steady drizzle. I was too shy to move at first, and it was more of a swaying song than a dancing one, but Jamie twirled me around a few times as I laughed, then I did the same to him. I wanted to follow his lead and let myself go, but I was too aware of him, of us, of the mud squishing between my toes, of my T-shirt clinging to my chest. During the musical interlude, he placed his hands on my waist, and I rested mine on his shoulders, and we weren't moving much anymore, simply looking at each other.

It was the prom dance I never got to have.

Jamie brought his lips to my ear. "*The hundred thousand waits that / are in your gaze and mine*," he whispered.

The interlude slowed, and just when it seemed the song might fade out, the tempo picked up, the music started to crescendo, and Thom Yorke ratcheted it up. As he sang an impassioned "*and one day I am gonna grow wings, a chemical reaction*," Jamie bent down and kissed me at last.

* * *

I was flying when I got home. I couldn't stay still, I paced, played "Let Down" on repeat, whirled in circles, lay on my bed kicking my legs and releasing cries of happiness into my pillow.

In my clandestine celebrations, there was one key element missing. For nearly three years, I'd shared my thoughts, my wishes, my family, with Farah. Being in love was a private matter between two people, but until someone close to you bore witness to it, it didn't seem as real. I wanted to celebrate it with her, I wanted her to see how happy I was, happier than I'd ever believed possible.

Until I told her, it wouldn't feel complete.

II.

The Night of Union

Twelve

THOUGH CLOVER CREEK HAD a perfectly decent high school, my mother insisted that for my sophomore year I switch to Lincoln Prep, a prestigious private school in a town known for its Wall Street money and Republican voter base. Most students at Lincoln Prep were good looking and good athletes, got good grades, went on to join the popular fraternities and sororities on campus. I didn't fit into the Lincoln Prep mold, and I didn't have athletic ability or musical or acting talent or gaming skills, or anything else that could be used as social lubricant to gain acceptance by my peers.

After reviewing the extracurricular options, I attended a meeting of the LGBT/Straight Alliance, which consisted of five students sitting in a circle. I chose a seat next to Ian. He didn't look like a typical Lincoln Prep student. He was a little darker than me, and had high cheekbones and deep brown eyes that narrowed slightly, wore a cool ring on every finger. I immediately wanted to be his friend.

"Do I have something on my face?" he asked, and I realized I'd been staring.

In my nervousness, I said, "Are you half and half?"

Thankfully, Ian gave me a chance before writing me off as a racist idiot.

"Are you referring to my ethnicity, or how I take my coffee?" he replied.

"I'm so sorry," I told him. "I didn't mean it like that."

"It's okay," he said. "You're not the first to be curious, though no one's asked quite like you. My father's black, and my mother's Thai. How do you identify?"

"My parents are from Pakistan."

"Cool. But I meant your gender and sexual identity."

"Oh. Uh, I'm a female. And straight," I said, apologetically.

"Why did you decide to join this group?"

"Because I don't have much talent, and most of the kids in this school seem like they're from some no-acne, fat-free planet, and I needed to join an extracurricular, and I figured this would be the least judgmental," I admitted. "Sorry—I guess that's not a good enough reason. Maybe I should go."

He grinned. "Nah. It's a good enough reason for me, and I'm the president."

Ian became my first friend at Lincoln Prep. That happened to be the meeting in which the LGBT/Straight Alliance voted to abolish the Straight, but they let me stay.

Once, after a meeting, this girl Agatha asked me, "Isn't it boring, to be so *normative*?"

But at Lincoln Prep, I didn't feel normative. I felt invisible, except for my hair.

I saw Farah before she saw me. I was sitting with Ian and Danny in the window seat of the student lounge, which overlooked Lincoln Prep's grand, imposing main entrance. Ian and Danny were taking selfies of themselves to use as profile pictures for some new gay teen social networking site. They weren't happy with any of the photos, pronouncing themselves too fat, too skinny, too freckled, too big-nosed. I was staring out the window, listening to them repeat *Gross! Delete!* when I noticed Farah standing at the bottom of the marble steps. Her blue plaid uniform skirt hit her mid-calf; unlike the other girls, she hadn't hemmed it to a more fashionable length. Her hair was iron straight with deep blue streaks and she was wearing blue lipstick. I didn't even know they made blue lipstick.

She reminded me a bit of my mother—long face, elegant nose. She had a prominent widow's peak. Her eyeliner was so thick I could see it from here. She was striking. Beautiful.

I watched as she visibly exhaled, looking up at our school's pillared entrance.

Come on, I thought. If anyone can do it, it's you.

She squared her shoulders, and started to climb the stairs.

"Who is *that?*" Danny asked.

"Oooh," Ian said. "Love the hair, but not so sure about the lipstick."

"Yeah, what's it called, Hypothermia?" Danny riffed. "Delete."

"I like it," I said.

Danny elbowed Ian. "I think your friend has the hots for Hypothermia."

"You sure you're straight?" Ian teased.

"Strike a pose," I ordered, grabbing Ian's phone and taking a photo to get them to shut up.

I saw her next in pre-calculus. I was already at a desk in the back when she walked in. Our eyes met. The thick silver hoop through her left nostril was another indication that she could be South Asian. I was hoping she'd choose a desk near me but she opted for the front. When she introduced herself as Farah Haider, I knew she was Muslim. Another thing we had in common. Sort of.

Days passed, but she didn't hem her skirt. Most girls had theirs hit above the knee, the popular girls mid-thigh, a few, as Ian called it, "low-butt." My mother, whose definition of modesty for me was at or below the knee and well above the boob, had hemmed mine exactly knee length, not so cool, but not weirdo Amish like Farah.

Naturally, the students made fun of her, but she didn't seem to care. As far as I could tell, she wasn't engaging in any effort to make friends. I'd see her in the library, reading, or drawing in her notebook or on her arm, wearing these big silver headphones, bopping her head to the music. I wanted to be her friend but I didn't know how; I smiled at her a few times, but she barely smiled back.

In the middle of fall semester, I entered the auditorium for a school assembly and saw her in one of the back rows, surrounded by empty seats. She'd braided all of her blue streaks, it looked really cool. I walked down her row, pretending to read texts on my phone to make it seem less deliberate, and sat one seat away from her. For me, this was already an act of courage, and I was hoping she'd take it from there, but she kept her headphones on. She was reading a book. It was called *Tripping with Allah: Islam, Drugs, and Writing.*

She wasn't going to make this any easier. As I got up the nerve to say something, she sighed, slid her headphones down to her neck, stretched her arms forward, interlaced her hands, and cracked her knuckles loudly. Her wrists were even more hirsute than mine, back before I started epilating them every week.

She glanced at me.

Say something.

"My arms are hairy, too," I said. "Except I epilate them."

As she wrinkled her forehead, I realized too late that could be construed as an insult.

"Do you always lead like that?" she asked.

"Beginnings aren't my strong point," I admitted.

"I see. You know, you could try, Hi, my name's Shabnam, what's yours?"

"You know my name!" I exclaimed.

"Uh, you're in pre-calc with me. You messed up that logarithm question in class the other day."

"Oh. Yeah, that was me." Considering my father was a mathematician, you'd really think I'd be better at it.

"You're Muslim?"

"My mother is," I told her.

"What's your dad?"

"Weird."

She snorted. "And what about you?"

"Me? I'm . . . nothing."

"You can't be nothing. At minimum, you're a *Homo sapiens*."

"Well, yeah. What are you?" I asked.

"I'm Muslim," she answered.

"You don't seem it," I said.

"Check your bias," she replied. "Anyway, I'm more of a Muslim misfit."

"Cool," I said, though I wasn't quite sure what she meant by that.

"Are you queer?" she said. "I'm cool if you are, but I'm straight, and anyway I'm celibate until further notice."

"And I'm the token straight person in the LGBT Alliance."

"Ah. At least they don't call it the LGBT/Straight Alliance

like they used to. I swear this school is so twentieth century. And the uniforms? Girls in skirts, boys in pants? How misogynistic/gender normative can you get? How has this not been an issue before?" she demanded.

"I know," I said. "It's such a pain to have to shave your legs every day when its gets too warm for tights."

Farah gave me this strange look, and I marveled at the dramatic symmetry of her eyeliner, curving to a fine point a half inch beyond her lids.

"You keep shaving, Qureshi," she said. "I'm going to wear pants."

"But you're not allowed to."

"Who says? The Man? Are you going to fight the Man, or are you going to let him step on your face?"

"Uh . . . neither?"

She laughed. "Well, I'll fight for both of us then. Principal Stone better brace himself."

A few weeks later, Farah was wearing the same navy polyester chinos as the boys. After listening to her feminist argument, Principal Stone informed her that all female students were entitled to wear pants; all they had to do was fill out a dress code exception form. Farah argued there shouldn't even be the need for an exception, and Principal Stone told her she was welcome to start a student petition. She wrote up the petition and it got passed around. When it came back to her, only thirty-three people had signed it, someone had crossed out *Pants* and written

Hot Pants instead, and someone else had written *Long Live Easy Access Pussy!* across the top.

"Fuck this noise," Farah said. "I'm going to buckle down and focus on getting into Harvard."

Farah began spending a lot of time at my house, and was even allowed to sleep over because her mother assumed we were a good Muslim family like theirs. My mother wasn't at all perturbed by Farah's punk style or dyed hair. She was thrilled I'd become such good friends with a girl who was Pakistani, and Muslim, and excelled at school, and who made me happy. "You're like sisters!" she exclaimed. She even began referring to Farah as her second daughter. I don't know about sisters, but we quickly became best friends. You could have stuck Farah and me in a room with blank walls and we still would have had a blast, talking shit and laughing our asses off. I could never stand out from the crowd like she did, but I loved being her more "normal" sidekick. We became our own breed of Lincoln Prep misfits. I finally found somewhere I belonged.

As close as we were, we had some major differences. I was the only child of two working parents. My dad hardly spent any money except on books, my mother was frugal, our house was paid up, my parents could afford the Lincoln Prep tuition. I had my own car, a ten-year-old Honda Accord, and I got a two-hundred-dollar-a-month allowance. If I ever needed anything—a new laptop, etc.—all I had to do was ask. I'd only have to take out a partial loan for college, and my mother said they'd help me with the payments later on if needed. I didn't feel rich, especially compared to the kids at Lincoln Prep, but I never had to worry about money.

Farah, on the other hand, was one of four children. Her father worked as an engineer for the town she lived in, and it didn't pay much, and her mother was a stay-at-home mom who watched a lot of QVC. Her mother was always complaining that her dad didn't make enough, that he was lazy and unambitious, and her father would say that if she needed so much money she should go find a job herself. Sometimes, especially after a QVC shopping binge, their fights would turn nasty. Farah was at Lincoln Prep on full scholarship. Even though she was a talented artist who loved drawing, she wouldn't even consider art school because she never wanted to depend on someone else for money like her mother did, and because she wanted to make enough to help put her younger siblings through college. She was going to become a doctor, one thing about her that toed the line of a good Pakistani girl.

Farah also engaged deeply with her *deen*, or faith. She spent a lot of time thinking about Islam, which I didn't, except occasionally when my father went on a rant about the evils of Saudi Arabia and Wahhabism. Her family had been going to the same *masjid*, or mosque, regularly, for years. She prayed every day, didn't drink, wouldn't date, fasted during Ramadan. She also swore a lot, listened to punk music, wore combat boots outside of school, and wanted to pierce her lip except her mother, who wore hijab, could barely deal with her ever-changing hair color. Her mother would say things like, *What if you go to Harvard and then boys are too intimidated to marry you? You already look like a freak.*

One day, Farah told me she'd listened to a *Radiolab* episode about memory. "Do you know, the more you remember and talk about something, the less reliable your memory is about that particular thing?" she said. "Given what we know about how memory is so fallible and easily influenced, I don't understand why we're still following hadith. They're all he said/she said hearsay. Every time my parents fight, my dad will throw out with some stupid hadith about how the majority of people in hell will be women."

"Did the Prophet really say that?" I asked.

"No! That's the point. He didn't really say any of it. We don't know what he actually said, but centuries later Muslims are still trying to base their lives on it. There are a few hadith I like, though, like the Prophet saying that Allah told him, 'I was a hidden treasure and I wanted to be known.' It's kind of beautiful, though it does make Allah sound pretty egomaniacal."

"I don't get it," I said. "If you have so many questions, how can you believe?"

"I have so many questions *because* I believe," she replied.

I still didn't get it, but it didn't matter, at least not until our senior year. Over winter break, Farah went to visit her cousins in San Francisco, buying her ticket with money she'd earned the summer before. She flew to the West Coast with magenta-colored hair, and returned with every strand covered by a black headscarf.

When I saw her enter school, my mouth fell open. We'd been in touch over break, but she hadn't mentioned this at all. I knew that a piece of cloth shouldn't make a difference, that she was still the same person underneath, but it did make a difference. Even though she was still wearing her dramatic eyeliner and blue lipstick, she looked, well, *religious*. And religious wasn't cool.

"Surprise," Farah said, frowning as she adjusted her scarf's folds around her face and neck. "How does it look?"

"Great," I lied.

"No, it doesn't," she said, touching the back of her scarf, where it kind of poofed out in the middle, as if covering a large bun. "My cousin told me it would take a while to get the hang of tying it, and figure out what style I liked. I've been YouTubing it, but I still spent half an hour this morning putting it on, I stabbed myself with a pin twice, and it looks terrible. Plus, if I want to cover my whole widow's peak, I'd have to wear my scarf like, halfway down my forehead."

She was exaggerating, but not by much. "Can't you ask your mother for help?"

"Ha. She's super pissed that I continue to dress like a freak even though I wear hijab."

"But . . . why did you decide to wear it?"

"I always figured I would, if it felt right."

She'd never told me that.

"Qureshi? You okay?" Farah asked.

I was relieved when the bell rang, giving me an excuse not to answer.

Farah told me she met her cousin's new wife in San Francisco, a badass spoken word poet who wore hijab, and she'd told Farah she didn't have to change her look at all, she could just add hijab to it, that there were people who were going to judge her no matter what she did—if she wore hijab, if she didn't—so all she could do was be true to herself. Inspired, Farah had worn it with her one day, and then decided not to take it off.

A lot of kids at Lincoln Prep hadn't even known Farah was Muslim, unless they took a history class with her or paid attention to the Allah pendant she sometimes wore on a black leather cord around her neck. The students gave her a harder time when she first showed up in her unhemmed skirt than when she started wearing hijab. Some of them even made it a point to be nice to her, as if to prove they weren't prejudiced. A lot of them asked her dumb questions. Since I was her best friend, sometimes I got asked dumb questions, like does she have cancer, do her parents force her to wear it, did her hair fall out because she dyed it so much.

"What's up with the headscarf?" Ian asked me.

"Delete," Danny said.

Farah got asked those questions and a hundred thousand others—if she showered in it, if she slept in it, if she still combed her hair, if she was going to have an arranged marriage, if she'd started wearing it because she thought it might make her stand out on her college applications.

The headscarf made a difference to Farah, too. She was conscious of it, always tugging at it, adjusting it, and she became more subdued, like she was trying to figure this new Farah out. Before, people knew her as the feminist in pants or the girl with chameleon hair, but now when they saw her, the first thing they thought of was that she was Muslim.

Initially, the new Farah responded to all the mostly dumb questions nicely, worried that if she was too rude or sarcastic they might walk away with a bad impression of a religion that already had enough negative press. But this also meant she had to suppress her natural impulses, and it made her less fun. I knew I should be patient, give her time to figure this all out, but I wanted my best friend back, the one who didn't take crap from anyone.

Plus, I hated this new kind of attention, where everything was about Islam. I was tired of having people ask me if I was Muslim too, of having to explain that I wasn't really, and feeling guilty about it, like I'd betrayed Farah, even though I'd never signed up for any of this.

When Farah confessed how exhausting this was for her, or showed me the comments over a photo she'd posted on a hijabi Tumblr, where a bunch of people had criticized her formfitting long black dress and red-laced black combat boots and heavy eyeliner and blue lipstick, saying it wasn't Islamic, one guy called *jamesdeen786* even calling her a *ho*jabi, I'd say, "So stop wearing hijab."

After a while, Farah stopped complaining to me. Instead, she withdrew, bit by bit. I knew I should reach out, bring her in for a tight embrace, tell her I loved her no matter what, but I was annoyed at how she'd pulled this without even a warning, that she hadn't considered how this would affect our friendship, had taken her *deen* to a place I couldn't follow.

And, deep down, I kind of agreed that the headscarf was a symbol of oppression. It wasn't like men had to cover every strand of their hair. I'd heard my father rant about how the Quran was revealed to a particular people at a particular time and needed to be adapted as times changed, how all religions were controlled and interpreted by men and thus backward and misogynist. (He'd be on the couch saying this as my mother was cooking dinner in the kitchen.) It seemed to me that, on some level, feminist Farah was submitting to the patriarchy.

After Farah started wearing hijab, I even read some Muslim feminist writers who explained that the Quran didn't actually direct women to cover their hair, that it was a misinterpretation of the text combined with the adoption of patriarchal cultural traditions. When I presented these arguments to Farah, she sighed and said she'd read all of their books and more, and that she wasn't wearing it because she believed it was a commandment from Allah. Yes, she was wearing it as an expression of her faith, but for her it was as much political as it was religious;

because we lived in a society where both Muslims and women were constantly objectified, this was her way of subverting that objectification; she was fighting the Man, she was making a statement, she was continuing her punk Muslim rebellion.

But I still didn't understand.

Our friendship was beginning to fray, but neither of us was doing much about it. Then, one day, a lanky junior named Ashish stopped her in the parking lot to ask, "Hey, can I ask you something?"

I could sense Farah's internal, *not again* sigh.

Taking her silence for an affirmative, Ashish asked, "I don't understand why the Muslims don't tell the terrorists to stop?"

For Farah, this was some kind of breaking point, the end of nice.

She clapped her hand over her mouth. "Oh. My. God. You are so right! Hold on—" She took out her phone and pretended to dial. "Hello, Terrorists? Hi! Can you please stop blowing stuff up, it's becoming a real drag. You will stop? No more beheadings, no more suicide bombs? Awesome, thanks! What? Can I stop US hegemony? Sure, no problem, I'll make sure it's over by tomorrow. All right, later! Holy shit, Ashish, thanks to you I just saved the world."

Ashish stared at her for a moment, then muttered something under his breath and shuffled away.

"So much for brown solidarity," I said.

"That felt so good," Farah proclaimed. "I didn't change my

style for hijab, I'll be damned if I change my personality, too."

"But you should be careful," I cautioned. "You don't want people to think you're making light of terrorism, either."

"Fuck them and their bigoted rhetoric. You don't hear me asking Ashish why he didn't stop right wing Hindus from burning Muslims alive in Gujarat!"

"Wasn't that a long time ago?"

"It's still happening—God, Qureshi, whose side are you on? You know what, forget it." Farah shook her head. "I gotta go home."

"I thought you were sleeping over," I said.

"Nah, not today."

"But how will you get home?"

"I'll take the bus."

"You mean two buses."

"Well, not all of us gets to have their own car," Farah said.

"My car is a piece of crap!" I protested.

She shook her head. "You're so clueless sometimes."

"What are you talking about?"

"You know how I told you since I started wearing hijab people stand farther away from me, especially guys? Well, guess what? So do you."

"I do not," I protested.

"Really? Look at where you are right now."

She was right; I used to walk around practically linking arms with her and now I was standing a good three feet away. I quickly closed the gap between us. A few crumbs of the chocolate chip cookie she'd had at lunch were caught in the neck folds of her scarf, but now was definitely not a good time to point this out.

"If I was doing it, it wasn't consciously," I said.

"Jesus Christ," she said.

"Don't you mean Prophet Isa?"

It was a lame joke, and Farah didn't laugh.

"I'll stand closer to you now," I promised.

"When I was in San Francisco, thinking about how it would be to come back to this bastion of white privilege in hijab, you know what gave me comfort?" Farah said. "That my best friend Shabnam Qureshi would be there for me."

"Farah . . . I want to be there for you. But it doesn't even seem like this hijab thing is making you happy. I mean, sure, maybe people aren't objectifying your body or whatever, but aren't they objectifying you as a Muslim?"

"But I am a Muslim. I'm proud to be Muslim." She threw her hands up. "And I'm done defending myself."

"Wait," I pleaded.

"What?"

There was one cure for everything. "Ye Olde donuts?"

"Not today," she said.

I was going to call out to her, but then I thought, fuck her and her holier-than-thou attitude. I survived before her, I could do it again.

That was the beginning of the end.

* * *

Each year the seniors held a big charity drive, and the next afternoon we had a senior class meeting to vote on which charity to support. A list of the charities left in the anonymous suggestion box had been printed out and posted on the senior lounge bulletin board. One of them was Playgrounds for Palestine. It was easy to guess whose that was.

The senior lounge seating consisted of three couches and one long table with chairs. It was an unspoken rule that the popular kids had first dibs at the couches, the rest of us sitting on the chairs or on the windowsill or on top of the pool table. The nicest couch, a soft burgundy leather one that some alum had gifted last year, was considered the best seat in the house, reserved for people like Natasha and Amelia and Ryan.

When I walked into the lounge for the meeting, I saw Farah sitting in the center of the burgundy couch, headphones on, arms folded over her backpack, looking determined. What was she trying to prove? I thought. Both spaces on either side of her were empty, but I didn't dare trod on the territory of the popular kids. Plus, the couch was in the center of the room, so if I sat next to her everyone would be staring at us the whole time.

As I walked over to the pool table, I avoided eye contact with Farah. People kept arriving, the popular kids becoming pissed that she'd taken their spot. I heard Natasha say, "Who does she think she is?" I was glad she had her headphones on so she couldn't hear. No one sat next to her.

Enter Ryan D'Ambrosio III.

"Out of my way, turds," he said, gesturing with his lacrosse stick and surveying his seating options. He shrugged, plopped down on the couch next to Farah, and spread his legs wide.

"Hey," he said, lifting one of Farah's headphones and speaking loud enough for everyone to hear, "you don't have a bomb in that backpack, do you?" Then he nudged her like she was in on the joke, cried, "*Allahu Akbar*!" and pretended to machine gun the rest of the room, a few people keeling over backward in fake death.

Everyone laughed, not because it was funny, but because it was Ryan's role to make dumb jokes, and ours to laugh at them.

I didn't laugh for very long, though, and I was hoping Farah hadn't noticed. I thought she might respond to Ryan with sarcasm, like she had with Ashish, but Farah said nothing the entire meeting, sat there frozen, eyes wide, jaw clenched, the kind of face you make when you're trying hard not to cry.

I voted for Playgrounds for Palestine, as if that could make everything all right.

Thirteen

FARAH'S LITTLE BROTHER MOHI, short for Mohammed, answered the door, holding up the brim of his adult-sized NY Mets cap with one finger so he could see. Mohi had a cute bowl cut and an adorable, innocent face. You'd never guess he was the one who'd snuck into Farah's bedroom and spread peanut butter inside her underwear.

"*Salaam alaikum*," he greeted me.

"Nice hat," I told him.

"I'm going to be a pitcher for the Mets one day," he announced. "*Inshallah*."

"That's awesome," I said. "Is Farah home?"

"No."

"Do you know where she is?"

"Summer camp."

"What summer camp?"

"At the *masjid*. You want to try my hat on?"

"Maybe next time. Can you tell me how to get there?"

"You don't know how to get to the *masjid*?"

"I don't go to the *masjid*, and even if I did, it wouldn't be this one."

"It's that way," Mohi replied, pointing left.

"Thanks, that's very helpful," I said.

"You're welcome!" he said.

I smiled. "I was being sarcastic."

"What's sarcastic?"

"Your sister Farah, most of the time. All right, wish me luck."

"Luck!" Mohi called out, waving from the door.

I thought of Jamie as I opened Google Maps, wondering what he would do if he were ever in a foreign suburbia and needed to find the nearest *masjid*. Not that he'd ever be in that position, but still.

The *masjid* was a nondescript, boxy, two-story white building, the only Muslim architectural elements a portico of three rounded arches and the Quranic calligraphy over the entrance. I was dressed in a short-sleeve V-neck shirt, but luckily I didn't have to go inside; the campers were all behind the *masjid*, playing in the large, fenced-in field.

I walked through the gate that led to the field. A boys' soccer match was in progress, the pinnies of the opposing teams lighter and darker shades of green. A young man with a neatly trimmed beard and hip-hop baggy jeans was yelling orders at them from one corner. His team must have scored the point, because he cried out, "*Subanallah*!" and did a little shimmy.

The girls were at the farther end. I walked along the edge of the metal fence, stepping over several cigarette butts along the way. A dozen or so girls were holding bows and arrows, standing across from a line of round plastic targets set upon metal tripods. They looked around middle school age, and three were wearing their hijab turban style, which I guessed was in emulation of Farah, who'd started wearing her hijab that way right before we graduated. Today she was wearing a peacock blue turban, a black, high-neck, long-sleeve linen dress with black leggings, and black boots with blue laces.

The girls were listening intently to Farah, who was pacing between them and their targets, her hands clasped behind her back.

"Maybe it's that old lady who gave you a pitying look at the grocery store because she thinks you're some oppressed woman, maybe it's that kid in school who asked you if there was a bomb in your backpack, maybe it's the neighbor's pit bull that always tries to sniff your crotch when you have your period! Whatever, whoever, that bull's-eye is it! Remember, you are strong! You are brave! You are riot grrrls!" Farah got out of the way and lifted her arms. "All right, my Katnisses, ready, aim, fire!"

The arrows started flying in every direction, including one

that whizzed by Farah's head, but she didn't flinch, because she was too busy staring at me.

"How did you know I was here?" she asked.

"Mohi told me. They aren't worried you'll be a bad influence on the girls? Half of them are already in turbans."

"My dress may be controversial, but I'm still going to Harvard. Anyway, I'm only subbing for the week."

"Sister Farah?" One of the girls, whose mustache reminded me I should pick up some more bleach cream on the way home, called out. "Do you think you can show us how we actually *shoot* a bow and arrow?"

"I'm here for moral support," Farah answered. "If you have technical questions, ask Siri. Now keep practicing!" She turned back to me, arching one eyebrow, her silver eye shadow shimmering in the sun. "Why are you here?"

"I have to tell you something, and I wanted to say it in person."

"Oh." Farah unfolded her arms. "Go ahead."

"I'm in love, Farah!" I burst out. "I'm totally, madly in love!"

I was hoping for a show of enthusiasm, but instead she looked a little hurt. "Are you okay?" I asked.

"Yeah," she said. "So you're in love. *Al-hamdz.*" That was short for *al-hamdulillah*, praise be to Allah. "Who's the lucky man?"

"His name is Jamie." I summed up our glorious history in a few sentences, Victoria's Secret, farmers' market, pie shack, kiss. "God, I was so happy when he kissed me, it's torture to like someone and worry they won't like you back. Whenever he touches me, I feel this ecstatic shiver. When I kiss him it's like my whole body is on fire. It literally leaves me breathless. I always thought that was some cheesy romance novel thing but it actually happens! I'm like a moth about to enter the flame—"

"Shut up, Qureshi."

"What?" I said, stung.

"We can't talk about this here. You're standing on *masjid* property, close to a bunch of twelve-year-olds."

"So let's meet up somewhere where we can talk about this. Plus, I want you to meet him."

"We've been on radio silence since graduation, and now you want me to meet your new boyfriend?" Farah said. "Why?"

It gave me a thrill to hear her refer to Jamie as my boyfriend.

"Because he's important to me, and so are you. I miss you. Ever since I met Jamie, I've been dying to talk to you about it, and it's been really hard," I said.

"Sister Farah! Does sharting break *wudu*?" one of the turbaned girls called out, and the others burst out laughing.

"Sassy," I said.

Farah sighed. "I gotta get back to these pimple factories."

She clearly had no interest in meeting the love of my life. Why would she, when she refused to open herself up to even the possibility of love.

"Okay. See you soon, I guess."

As I walked away, she yelled, "Fine."

I turned back. "Fine what?"

"Fine, I'll meet him. Text me later."

I had to restrain myself from shimmying back to the car.

Fourteen

NOW THAT JAMIE AND I were an item, we'd forsaken Mrs. Joan Milton's bench for the shack, talking and laughing and making out in our private cocoon that smelled of flour and butter and fruit and sugar, of all the sweet, good things in life.

Lovely though it was, the shack wasn't very comfortable for hooking up. We couldn't both lie down without being half on top of each other, which sounds great except the floor was hard and had nails poking out of it. When we sat up against the wall, we had to keep our knees bent. Plus it was hot, and at some point even Jamie started sweating, though his sweat smelled like pie. Before opening up for business, I'd have to sanitize my face, my neck, and my pits with baby wipes.

But we managed pretty well with the space we had. Yesterday, he'd lain down lengthwise and placed his head in my lap.

At first, I'd been nervous I might fart, or that maybe my crotch smelled weird, or that there were boogers in my nose. But then I saw Jamie smiling up at me so casually, as if he'd been lying in my lap for years, that I quickly relaxed, enjoying the weight of his head, playing with his awesome hair, which had so much body it practically had a life of its own.

The next day, when he put his head on my lap, the nightingale didn't tremble once.

I smiled down at him, brushing the hair from his forehead. "I got another poem from my father."

"A ghazal?" he asked.

"No, another free form by Faiz."

He reached up, wound a curl around his finger. "Where's my ghazal?"

"It's coming," I promised. "Now do you want to hear the poem or not?"

"I'm all ears."

This time, I had it memorized.

"So this is an excerpt from 'The Desert of Loneliness,' another poem by Faiz Ahmed Faiz, translated, of course, by my father."

In the desert of loneliness, beneath the dust and weeds of distance,
Blossom the roses and jasmine of being by your side

From somewhere very close rises the heat of your breath
Slowly smoldering in its own fragrance

Far across the horizon the shining dew of
Your beloved gaze falls, drop by drop

With such love, o life of the world, has your memory
Placed its hand on the face of my heart
Though it's still just the dawn of our separation
It feels that the day of exile has passed, and the night of union is already here

"*With such love, o life of the world, has your memory / Placed its hand on the face of my heart*," he repeated. "If it's so beautiful in English, what's it like in Urdu?"

"Must be pretty darn good," I said, tracing the scar between his collarbones. The one on his hand was the most visible, but if you looked carefully, you'd find the others. He'd told me an art major he'd dated at U. Wisconsin Madison had drawn red lines on his naked self, connecting all of his scars, and taken a photo for her senior art thesis, calling it "Map of Old Wounds." I wished I was artsy and cool like her. I wished Jamie and I had more time together. I wished this summer would never end.

But, unless Jamie decided to stay after the shack closed, we had ten days left.

"So when do I get to eat some Pakistani food?" he asked.

"What do you want to eat?"

"Whatever the lady brings me."

"Well, what do you like?" I asked.

"I don't know, I've never tried it."

"Have you had Indian food? It's a lot like North Indian."

"I've hit the lunch buffet at Mirch Masala in Madison a few times, it's pretty good. I really dig their lamb biryani."

"That's a little complicated to make, I think."

"My other favorite is chicken tikka . . ."

"Chicken tikka masala. My mother doesn't make that. She says it's not even Indian."

"So my favorite Indian dish isn't really Indian? Figures." He sat up, and kissed the tips of my fingers. "I've got a lot to learn, huh? I'm lucky I have such a beautiful teacher."

I died of happiness every time he looked at me with those honey hazel eyes and called me beautiful. He could do so every day of my life and I was certain it would never get old.

He kissed me and I kissed him back harder. His hand slipped under my shirt, his fingers searing my skin. I sucked in my stomach fiercely, and as his hand moved up to my chest, I regretted my choice of cotton bra, old and saggy and stretched out. I needed underwear that could actually be called lingerie.

"Is this okay?" Jamie asked, his hand still cupping my breast.

"Yes," I replied.

"I should check the time," he said.

"Noooo."

"I don't want to stop either, MD, but I made a promise to Aunt Marianne that we'd always open on time."

It was almost four, as always. As Jamie helped me up, he said,

"Listen, I know you're from a different culture, so you can tell me to stop whenever."

It struck me as a weird thing to say, because yes, my parents were Pakistani, but I thought it was pretty obvious that, despite my occasional self-deprecating inner monologue, I was as eager to hook up as he was. I'd already decided I'd have sex with him, if we got that far, because I loved him and he was the sweetest, coolest guy I'd ever met and I'd be lucky to lose my virginity to him. Plus I wouldn't have to start college a virgin.

"Thanks. But you should know I really love kissing you," I said.

"And I love kissing you," Jamie replied, his lips traveling across my cheek to meet mine.

I moaned, quietly but decisively, to indicate how into it I was.

"Goodbye, Morning Dew," he whispered, the warmth of his breath tingling in my ear.

In the desert of loneliness, beneath the dust and weeds of distance,
Blossom the roses and jasmine of being by your side

My rose, my jasmine, my Jamie.

Bliss.

Fifteen

FARAH WAS EASY TO spot; she was the sole hijabi in the mall food court, dressed in black from head to toe, except for her boots' turquoise laces. As I came closer, I noticed her scarf was subtly patterned with raised fists.

"Greetings," I said. "Sorry I'm late, my mom dropped me off and you know how slow she drives." I didn't bother explaining that I had my mom drive me so I could have Jamie give me a ride home. "Plus, we made a pit stop."

Farah pointed to the white paper bag dangling from my hand. "Please tell me that's Ye Olde donuts."

"You are correct, madam," I said, then clapped my hand over my mouth. "Shit! I forgot it's Ramadan!"

"Except it doesn't matter because I'm on my period," Farah

declared with a finger snap. "*Al-hamdz*! I'm so happy you brought Ye Olde. I've been sitting here inhaling Cinnabon for the past ten minutes and was about to cave and buy one."

"Please. Cinnabon? That's like sacrilege. Allow me to present chocolate cream, raspberry jam, and vanilla lavender," I said, ceremoniously laying the three donuts in a line on top of the bag.

"Beauties!" Farah exclaimed. "Did you say vanilla lavender? When did Dino start making bougie donuts? Will you split that and the chocolate with me?"

We each picked one up and broke it in two. Mine split unevenly, one half getting most of the chocolate cream. I graciously handed the better half to Farah, hoping she'd notice.

"How's our fabulous donut maker?" she asked, licking a dollop of chocolate cream from her finger.

"He's happy to see me but sad you're not with me."

"Ah, Dino. I miss him. And where is Prince Charming?"

"He texted that he was running late and would meet us here," I told her. "I really like the turban look, by the way."

"Because it feels a little more African and a little less Muslim?" she replied wryly. "You know, some Muslims don't like it precisely because of that. They think it doesn't look Muslim enough, whatever the hell that means."

"God, you really can't win, can you?"

"When do women ever win, anywhere?"

I thought about this. "Scandinavia?"

"Yeah," she said. "But then again, it's not so great to be

Muslim in Scandinavia."

"So we're screwed."

"Unless we change the world."

"Are those black power fists on your scarf?"

"Does it look okay?" Farah said, smoothing the top fold. "I swear, I spend more time on my hijab than I ever did on my hair."

"That's because your hair is straight. Where did you find it?"

"My hijab? My friend told me about this website that sells badass scarves."

I thought it was weird she didn't use her friend's name, given that I'd met most of them. "Which friend?"

"Shahnaz. I met her through the internet—she has this awesome Tumblr blog."

"Shahnaz?" I exclaimed.

"What?"

"That's so close to my name."

"Because it shares the first syllable?"

I folded my arms. "Does she wear hijab?"

"Yes."

"You're replacing me," I accused her.

"You, Qureshi, are irreplaceable."

I smiled. "It's so nice to be here with you."

"Why? Because I'm fun again?"

She said it like she was joking, but I knew there was more to it. After months of estrangement, here we were, behaving like

BFFs again, except we still hadn't discussed what happened. I hadn't brought it up because things were going pretty well and I didn't want to risk ruining it. I was hoping it would resolve itself with time. But when there's so much left unsaid, it takes more than the bigger half of the donut to set things right.

"There's Jamie." I stood up and waved, which I promptly felt dumb doing, because it seemed overeager and it wasn't that big a food court. He was in his usual attire of Converse and rolled-up jeans, with the addition of a hunter-green fedora.

"Greetings, ladies," Jamie said, tipping his hat. His gaze lingered on Farah; I hadn't told Jamie she wore hijab. I didn't want him to come with any preconceived notions about who she was.

"Greetings, Homo sapiens," Farah said. "Pull up a chair."

He grabbed a chair from a neighboring table, flipped it around, and sat on it backward, his fingers tap-dancing along the metal bars of the backrest.

"That"—Jamie pointed at Farah and made a circling motion around her face—"is a very cool scarf."

"Thanks," Farah said. "I wish I could say the same about your style of wearing jeans."

Not everyone appreciated Farah's humor, but Jamie didn't miss a beat. He stuck his leg out. "What?" he said, pretend-shocked. "Are you saying I'm not the height of fashion?"

Farah nodded slightly, and I knew she was thinking, *at least he can play*. They were off to a good start.

She gestured at the table's centerpiece—a fluffy, golden, fresh-raspberry-jam-engorged donut. "Would you like to sample the greatest donut in the world?"

"Who could say no to that?" Jamie said.

I frowned. I'd wanted to be the one to offer Jamie his very first Ye Olde donut experience. I was the one who bought them, after all. But I told myself that was stupid, and Farah and I leaned forward in anticipation of this life-changing moment. Jamie took a big bite, and immediately his eyes lit up. "*Ummmmmmm*," he said, the same kind of noise he'd made yesterday when I'd finally got up the nerve to rest my hand on the crotch of his jeans and feel the erection throbbing inside.

"I got an idea for a meme," Farah said. "We can go around offering random people Ye Olde donuts and capture their initial reaction."

"Love at first bite," I said.

"It's like my tongue had an orgasm," Jamie said.

"Donut porn," Farah said, and he laughed.

"I bought them," I told Jamie.

"Thanks, Morning Dew."

"Morning Dew?" Farah repeated.

"It's Jamie's nickname for me," I explained. "It's because my name means morning dew in Persian."

"Are you Persian?" Jamie asked Farah.

"Nope, I'm Pakistani, like your girl over here. You ever dated a brown girl before?" Farah said.

"Yeah, but she was Hispanic," Jamie replied.

"Well, you know what they say, once you go brown you never go back. Welcome to the dark side," Farah said, raising her coffee cup.

"Thanks," he said. "I like your necklace."

Farah had made it in a woodworking workshop she'd taken during Senior Art Week, polished crescents of reclaimed wood hanging unevenly from a thin braided cord. The instructor had told her she should consider working with her hands. She'd taken it as a sign she should become a surgeon.

"Thanks. I made it," Farah told Jamie.

"Really? Wow."

"Farah's an awesome artist but she's going to be a doctor," I said.

"Oh?" Jamie replied. "How come?"

"Because I'll be readily employable, and earn a generous salary," Farah responded.

"What about helping people?" Jamie asked.

"Secondary," Farah replied.

I didn't think it was that funny, but Jamie laughed so hard his fedora fell off. I retrieved it for him, watching longingly as he ran his hands through his locks before putting it back on. I felt Farah looking at me. I could tell something was bothering her. Maybe she was jealous of me because I was in love. I'd be jealous of her if she was.

Jamie drummed his palms against the edge of the table. "So,

what's the plan? Are we mall ratting it at the food court all day?"

"Please. If I smell any more Cinnabon I might hurl," Farah said.

"So what should we do?" he wondered.

"Well, I was thinking of smoking a joint," Farah said.

"What?" I said. "Since when do you smoke pot?"

"Since I was in San Francisco with my cousins."

"But you started wearing hijab in San Francisco!"

"So?"

"So how can you do both? Isn't it forbidden?"

"The Quran doesn't forbid marijuana. It forbids wine. Wine was considered high class, a luxury. Hashish was for the 'losers,' the weirdos, the misfits, the wanderers, the dervishes and scholars. Why do you think so many Sufi mystics smoked it? People have always used it to bring themselves closer to truth, closer to Allah."

"Is that why you use it?" Jamie inquired.

"Sometimes. Sometimes I just smoke and watch a movie," Farah said.

"And you don't think it makes you a bad Muslim?" I pressed.

"I think it makes me a *better* Muslim," she replied.

I wanted to ask her what her hijabi friends at the *masjid* would think about that, but I already knew.

"You know, Morning Dew's been teaching me about Sufi mystics," Jamie informed her.

"Is that so?" Farah said, genuinely surprised.

"My dad's been teaching me about Urdu poetry, which is inspired by Sufi poetry," I explained. "Well, up till now we've pretty much only read Faiz."

"He's great!" Jamie proclaimed.

Farah nodded, impressed by Jamie's enthusiasm. "Sounds like it."

"So are we smoking?" Jamie said. "I'm down."

"Morning Dew?" Farah asked.

The name definitely didn't sound as nice when she said it.

Fifteen minutes later, we got into Jamie's minivan and drove to an empty corner of the mall parking lot, parking against the fence so we could only be approached in three directions. Farah's joint was already rolled, concealed inside a small odor-resistant container she'd bought off the internet. We sat on the hood of the car, and Farah lit the joint and took a long, smooth drag. I was so nervous when she passed it to me that I passed it right on to Jamie, who took an even longer drag, which culminated in one small cough and a shit ton of smoke.

I took the joint from Jamie and held it between my fingertips, hoping it wasn't obvious I hadn't done this before. After inhaling deeply, I erupted into a crazy coughing fit, my upper body convulsing. So much for playing it cool. Farah started pounding my back, Jamie rubbed my leg. My fit ended with a snort, which I tried to cover up with a fake cough.

I felt weirdly light, like a strong breeze might blow me away. Wanting to connect with something solid and windproof, I pressed my palms against the hood of the minivan, imagining myself an extension of its steel. I was acutely aware of Jamie's hand, still resting on my thigh. I was made of steel, but that steel was smoldering.

We must have been silent for only a minute or so, but it felt like ten. During this slow passage of time, I become aware of all kinds of things, the patterns in the asphalt, the serpentine sizzle of summer heat, the whir of distant traffic.

"Good stuff," Jamie said.

"*Kaisi ho*, Qureshi?" Farah asked.

"Fine," I assured her. "Really good."

Jamie offered me the dwindling joint, but I shook my head; I'd taken two hits now and was flying, so he passed it on to Farah.

"How did you get the crazy scar?" Farah asked him.

"This?" Jamie said, holding his hand up. "I punched through a window."

Farah glanced at me, signaling, *did you know this?* But I didn't, because I'd never asked.

"You punched a window?" I said. "Why?"

"I got in a fight with my stepfather."

"You have a lot of beef with your stepfather?" Farah said.

"Nah, not anymore. It was in high school, and he had a right to be pissed—I got arrested for trespassing. He's actually a decent guy—my mother married him because he was the opposite of my real dad—nice, dependable, steady job, drove reeeeeeeal slow. She thought he'd make a good father figure.

But even though I was still a kid when they married, I could tell she didn't love him, at least not the way she loved my dad. She thought he was kind of boring. Sometimes when he was telling one of his long-winded stories I'd catch her rolling her eyes when she thought no one was looking. I used to look down on her for marrying this guy she didn't love, but I get it now. She had a kid, she was scared. But I never want to be like that. I never want to be bored."

I realized this was the most I'd heard Jamie share about his personal life.

"Yeah, man," Farah agreed. "I never want to be in a marriage like my parents. After my parents' most recent blowout, I asked my mother how she married my father. She said it had come down to two engineers with a green card, and she told her parents she liked my dad better because in his photo he was wearing two different-colored socks. She thought it was cute."

"It is kinda cute," I said.

"No it isn't!" Farah cried. "I mean, if you get a proposal from a guy in two different-colored socks, don't you think you ought to *investigate* a little before you decide to *marry* him? Like, is he color-blind? Is he lazy? Is it a fashion statement? Like what the fuck is going on?"

Jamie and I were both laughing, Jamie so hard he was lying back against the hood, kicking his heels against the bumper.

"Show me a marriage that isn't somehow depressing," Farah concluded, "and I'll show you a unicorn."

"Oh, come on," I said. "If you marry the right person, marriage can be awesome, right?"

"Qureshi, you hopeless romantic," Farah said. "It's all those rom-coms you watch with your mom."

"Don't forget Bollywood," I reminded her.

"I've never seen a Bollywood movie!" Jamie exclaimed. "Should we go see one? You think any are playing right now?"

"Of course there is, we're in New Jersey," Farah said. "But we're not going to one."

"Why not?" Jamie said.

Farah snorted. "Two stoned desi girls and a white guy going to a Bollywood movie? The theater will be full of aunties and uncles!"

Jamie shrugged. "They won't know you're stoned."

"But they'll know you're white," she pointed out.

Being in a crowded lobby surrounded by desi families sounded like a terrible idea. "And I'll know I'm stoned," I added.

"Yeah, we don't want Qureshi to start suddenly dancing like a chicken in the line for the bathroom."

"The last time I went to a Bollywood movie with my mom," I said, "I went to the bathroom, and someone let out a loud fart. And when I went to the sink, all the aunties were kind of looking at each other, thinking was it you, it was probably you, you totally look like you ate *chole* for breakfast."

Farah was cracking up, slapping her knee, and Jamie was watching us with a grin.

"What's *chole?*" he asked.

"Chickpeas," I said.

"Punjabi fart food," Farah said, and we cracked up again.

"Sorry," she told Jamie. "Sometimes Q and I can't help but dabble in a little bathroom humor. We come from a culture where your day can't properly begin until you take a good dump."

"I guess that's pretty on point," Jamie noted.

"Sometimes my dad will go into the downstairs bathroom with the *New York Times*," I said. "He'll be in there for like twenty minutes, and then bring the same paper to the table where we're all eating breakfast. So gross."

"So I guess that's a definite no on the movie?" Jamie said.

"Yeah, let's go. We can see if any of the aunties offer us their son's bio data." Farah began to imitate a Pakistani accent. "Look, there is Mahmood Haider's daughter, she is going to Harvard, so must be very smart, but wears hijab, so also must be good, religious girl."

"But why she has to dress in those garbage clothes?" I riffed.

"And *dehko*, what's on her necklace—skull! *Yeh ladki, shayad yeh ithni acchi nahin hai*," Farah continued.

"What does that mean?" Jamie asked.

"This girl, maybe she isn't so good after all," I translated.

Farah held up the nub of the joint. "Who wants the last drag?"

"It's all yours," I said.

As she exhaled, she said "What?" to me, and I realized that I'd been staring.

"It's so weird to see you smoke pot in hijab."

"Why?" Jamie asked.

"It's like . . ." I considered. "It's like if you saw a nun chugging a bottle of Jägermeister."

"Did you just compare me to an alky nun?" Farah exclaimed.

"You know what I mean," I said.

"What do you mean?" Jamie asked.

Farah sighed, leaning her elbows against the hood. "What Qureshi means is that the hijab is seen as a symbol of piety, and a girl wearing hijab is visibly Muslim, so people assume if you're wearing it you must be a model Muslim, very pious and straight, and most Muslims would say that you should aim to be a model Muslim, because you're now representing Islam to the whole world. *Par example*, if Qureshi is rude to a sales clerk, that sales clerk is going to think, 'That girl is such a bitch.' But if I'm rude to a sales clerk, she'll think, 'That Muslim girl is such a bitch.'"

"And you don't mind that pressure?" Jamie said.

Farah shrugged. "I'm not usually rude to sales clerks. They're poorly paid cogs in our screwed-up consumerist society."

"Yeah, man, we are so consumerist," Jamie agreed. "People forget what's really important. Like now, this moment, all of us together, the warm sun on our faces, the blue sky above, that's what's important. That's what really matters."

"I'll tell you what doesn't matter," Farah said. "QVC. An entire channel devoted to selling people shit they don't need."

"If you had to sell something on QVC, what would it be?" I asked.

"I don't even know," Farah said, and I could tell she was

thinking about something else. Her parents, probably.

After a few seconds of silence, Jamie said, "It must be hard, though, wearing that on your head. People must stare at you and stuff."

"Yeah, they stare. Though my friends who've worn hijab for a while say at some point you stop noticing it. You gotta keep walking with pride, like you belong on this street, or in this mall, or wherever, as much as anyone else. But the thing is, I get it from both sides. I told one of my hijabi friends who I thought was cool that I was going to see this awesome band, Rebel Antigone—they're great, it's a queercore band with two badass girls and this genderqueer lead singer who was trained in opera and has this killer voice, Qureshi, you'd probably hate them—but anyway she asked me if I was going to take my hijab off when I went to the club, and I was like why, and she said, you won't feel weird?, as if hijab and a punk show are fundamentally incompatible. Most of my hijabi friends would disapprove of me smoking weed. I don't know. I'm too Muslim for the non-Muslims, but not Muslim enough for the Muslims. And the weird thing is, I realized I've been trying to prove to people that I'm cool, that yeah, I don't drink and whatever but I'm smart and funny and extremely un-oppressed, but I wonder, at the end of the day, will they secretly think a girl in hijab can never be *that* cool simply because she wears hijab? But then I think, why does it matter what they think of me? I refuse to spend my life proving myself, not to the Muslims, not to the non-Muslims. I'm going to wear a headscarf and I'm going to pray and fast and I'm going to smoke ganja and I'm going to get into Harvard Medical School."

"Whoa, woman. I'd definitely put my money on you," Jamie said, looking a little awestruck. "And that band sounds cool—Rebel Antigone?"

"Yeah, you guys want to hear my favorite song by them?" she asked.

"Hell yeah!" Jamie replied.

She pulled her big headphones out of her messenger bag and plugged them into her phone. Jamie and I shared the headphones, my cheek pressed to his. The lead singer could definitely hold a note, and the screams were a lot more melodious than in most punk songs Farah had made me listen to.

Everyone stop trying to put a label on me
Everyone stop trying to put a label on me
I'm not a girl I'm not a guy
I'm not an x I'm not a y
I'm me
I'm me
If that's too vague
Then you're afraid
If that's too vague
Then you're afraid
But not me! Not me!
I'm the head I'm the tail

I'm Dorothy I'm the Wiz
I'm the Founding Fathers' anal snail
I'm the Statue of Liberty
I'm the heartbeat of
The land you love
I'm the home of the brave
And the free
The free! The free!
Saxophone!

Jamie, who'd been grooving the whole time, started rocking out to the frenetic wailing of a saxophone and something sounding like glass breaking. I let him have the other earpiece because he was obviously enjoying it so much.

"They're amazing!" he said, really loudly because of the headphones.

"Did he—she, they, say the Founding Fathers' anal snail?" I asked.

"The Founding Fathers' anal *grail*," Farah corrected me, as if that made any more sense.

Jamie took off the headphones.

"Sorry to cut this short," Farah apologized, sliding off the hood and tossing the headphones into her bag. "I gotta head. My mom needs to go shopping before *iftar*."

"Are you okay to drive?" I asked her.

"Yeah, I'm good."

I couldn't imagine driving right now. "Text me when you get back," I said.

"Will do. Later, kids."

"What's *iftar*?" Jamie asked after she left.

"Breaking the fast. It's Ramadan, the month of fasting."

"But didn't she eat a donut?"

"You're not supposed to fast when you're on your period," I said, blushing a little, not that Farah would care.

"Do you ever fast?"

"No. My mom used to, until she fainted at the office last year. Now she just prays a lot instead."

"Cool. Well, Morning Dew, what should we do now?"

We couldn't figure out where to go, so we drove down the street and pulled into a strip mall to figure out our next move. Jamie parked in front of the Amazing Chinese Restaurant, which had a dragon carved into its wooden door and paper lanterns hanging from its red awning.

As I was marveling at the audacity of the restaurant's name, Jamie played The National's "Fake Empire." He put his arm around me, reached for a curl that had escaped my ponytail, giving it a gentle tug as he coiled it around his finger.

I was relieved by this familiar, intimate gesture, a physical assurance that I was the one he liked, that it was my curl laying across his shoulder.

"What's her hair look like?" Jamie asked.

"What?"

"Your friend Farah. I was picturing short, maybe spiky?"

"No, it's long and straight, and very limp." I'd meant to say *very thick*, I really had. *Limp* sounded terrible, but I didn't correct myself.

"Why do you care?" I asked.

"Just curious. Are you all right?" Jamie asked, lifting my chin with his curl-wrapped finger.

"I'm all right," I said.

"Hey, should we see a movie?" he suggested. "Since we're across the street from the mall and we're still a little high . . ."

This reminded me I was supposed to see a movie with my mother. "I can't, I gotta be home in like an hour. But I think that gives us enough time for . . ." I spread my hands toward the windshield. "Amazing Chinese Restaurant!"

"That sounds—" he grinned.

"Don't say it don't say it—"

"Amazing!" he proclaimed, and I hit his chest playfully, and then we were kissing, so hot and heavy the windows turned steamy. When we broke away, I was sweaty and burning and a little surprised, because making out in the car was one of those seminal suburban high school moments I thought I'd never have, and not only had it happened, it had come so easily, so naturally, with a guy so cool.

Sixteen

I WAS STILL A bit high when I got home, and a little nervous about hanging out with my mother, but I was also flying from my amazing meal with Jamie and our second minivan make-out session. Being with my mother turned out to be super fun, because instead of focusing on what she wasn't (a liberal white mom who I could talk to about Jamie), I was able to relax and enjoy her for what she was: gentle and caring and a pretty good sport. I joked with her like I joked with Farah, tailoring my humor to her more refined nature. I even threatened to put a pea under her mattress to see if she'd feel it and she laughed and said "What nonsense," a phrase she'd stolen from my father, which got me cracking jokes about Dad, a source of endless comedic fodder, both imagined and real, like the time this auntie got a nose job and he asked her point-blank at a party what had happened to her face.

I hadn't seen my mother laugh so much in ages, and it made me guilty, because she should have had a couple of children to make her laugh and she had only one, who'd been doing a pretty miserable job of it.

After we got home from the cheesy rom-com, my mother hugged me and said, "I had such a lovely time. I hope we have more times like this before you leave for school."

Maybe the secret to getting along with your parents was marijuana.

I went to bed exhausted but unable to sleep; my mind was too wired, my thoughts lucid but tangled. I thought of rom-coms and Bollywood and how we loved them because they were so predictable, how strange it was to see Farah smoke weed in a hijab, how she so openly displayed her Muslim identity whereas if someone saw me they wouldn't know I was Muslim unless they asked, what Jamie said about his mother not loving his stepfather. I circled back to rom-coms, thinking about the universal happily ever after they had in common with Bollywood films, and I wondered if my parents loved each other, not the love you settle into because you've lived with a person for so long, but love like in a Faiz poem, love like in a Bollywood movie. Had they ever felt that way about each other? My mother had chosen him out of several suitors, but they hadn't really known each other before the wedding. Was my father capable of such a depth of emotion? And if he was, could he even express it? And if he wasn't, did that secretly upset my mother?

A little agitated, I turned on the bedside lamp, comforted by the sight of familiar objects: Big Muchli, the purple stuffed whale I'd had since I was four, on the pillow next to me, the Radiohead *OK Computer* poster over my desk, my clothes from today hanging over my desk chair. Everything in its right place.

I headed downstairs for a late-night snack. I'd very wisely stashed away a few Ye Olde donuts for moments like this. My mother had asked me to hide them from my father, but now, as I stood in the cold air of the open fridge, I couldn't remember where they were. Then I figured I would have picked the place my father was least likely to venture. Sure enough, they were at the back of the veggie drawer. Victorious, I grabbed the last two donuts, made two cups of tea, and knocked on my father's study, where I'd noticed the light was on.

"Entry," my father said.

I assumed he meant enter, and stepped inside.

I hadn't been in his study in years. Besides my bedroom, it was the only other space my mother didn't clean with her usual obsessive regularity. It smelled like old socks and Old Spice. There were papers everywhere, some stapled, some loose, some circularly imprinted by mugs, some bearing stains as yellow as urine. The wastebasket was overflowing. One wall had floor-to-ceiling built-in shelves, the lowest shelf home to a collection of leather-bound *Encyclopedia Britannicas* coated with a layer of dust you could spell your name in, the rest filled with books in Urdu and English in disorderly stacks. The recliner was similarly besieged, piled nearly to the top with books.

I paused, uncertain where to put his teacup; his desk was so cluttered you couldn't tell what it was made of.

"Here," I said, handing the cup to my father, who set it down without even bothering to look.

"Is this a Ye Olde donut?" my father asked.

"Don't tell Mom."

My father didn't reply; his mouth was already full.

I started removing books from the leather recliner so I could sit. Underneath the last book, a bright yellow math text called *An Introduction to Knot Theory*, was a highly fragrant brown-and-red striped sock. "Dad," I said, holding the sock up and away, "this is disgusting."

"What is?" he asked.

"Never mind," I said, opening the door and tossing it into the den for my mother to deal with later. "It's a wonder Mom hasn't murdered you, you know."

"Your mother abhors violence."

"I didn't mean it literally."

"Hmmph. Even so, the impossibility of the stated action undermines the efficacy of the hyperbole." My father said this in English, the language he used for such complex sentences, though that might also have been because I lacked the capacity to understand it in any other tongue.

"Yeah, okay. Listen, I have a question."

My father still had one bite of donut left. If he really liked something, he'd inhale it, but then hold off on the last bite, reluctant to finish, though I'd never seen this reluctance last more than a minute.

"Yes?" my father said.

I hesitated—was it wise to ask whether my father loved my mother? What did it matter? Even if he said yes, it wouldn't turn him into some expressive romantic, or even a normal guy. And what if he said no? What the hell would I do then? Did I really want to know all the ways in which my parents' marriage was depressing? Maybe not, but I felt like I'd plunged past the point of no return.

"So, we've been talking about love, and the lover, and the beloved, and longing, and all that, and I was wondering if you love Mom like that?" I asked.

My father blinked. "Like what?"

I tried again, more simply. "Do you love Mom?"

"Do I love your mother?"

"Do you?"

My father glanced at the last bit of donut, debated, put it down on top of his keyboard, picked it up again, ate it. I made a mental note to buy keyboard cleaner.

"Yes," he said. "I love your mother."

"Like the lover loves his beloved?"

"That kind of love is for Sufi mystics," my father said, "and poetry. That kind of love cannot be sustained between two mortals."

"Why not?" I asked.

"Because the love of the Sufi mystics, the love the poets mirror, is divine love. Humans are terribly flawed. Humans hurt each other. Humans become bored, humans become sick, humans are weak. When you are consumed by human love, it is like looking into a fire of your own making—you believe you are seeing your beloved, but it is a mere reflection of the intensity of your own emotion. When that fire cools, your beloved's true face, flawed, hopelessly mortal, is revealed. The only beloved who will not disappoint when you see his true face is Allah, because He is the source of all love, all light."

"I thought you were an atheist."

"I never said I was an atheist."

"So you believe in Allah?"

"That is a very complex question for such a late hour, though it is perhaps the most appropriate time to discuss such matters."

But I was finally starting to feel sleepy, and we were on the precipice of a long and potentially long-winded one-sided dialogue. "Okay, well, back to your love for Mom—so you're saying you can't really love a human because they will disappoint you."

"No, I am differentiating the love for the divine with the love for mortals."

"So you love Mom like a mortal."

"Yes."

"Meaning you know she will disappoint you because she's not Allah."

"Of course she will disappoint me. She is human, we are all flawed. It is the opposite—I don't expect her not to disappoint me. I don't expect not to disappoint her. I don't expect her to be Allah. That is the whole point."

"Okay, I get that two humans in love are inevitably going to disappoint each other. But I think you need to try harder not to disappoint her," I said.

"I don't understand."

"Why don't you help her with the dishes, buy her flowers? Mow the lawn before she asks you, without all your usual drama. It's really not that hard, Dad. I've mowed the lawn, twice."

I could see my father's face glazing over, as it did when my mother admonished him, and snapped my fingers in front of his face. He flinched, his glasses slipping off one ear.

"I'm serious," I told him. "I know your love is . . . pragmatic, but you should still tell her you love her, show her you care."

"But she knows I care."

"Really? I didn't think you cared about me until recently. And you definitely don't care about a lot of things that concern me."

"What concerns you?" my father said.

My mother may never murder him, but sometimes I thought *I* definitely could. "Even the fact you have to ask that—okay, what grade did I get in pre-calculus?"

"D?" my father ventured.

"A D? I know I'm not a math genius like you, but really? I got a B+, thank you very much. Anyway, my point is . . . Pardon my French, but love means sometimes acting like you give a shit."

My father frowned. "That's English, not French."

If I stayed, I was liable to hurl an *Encyclopedia Britannica* in his direction. Plus, I wasn't sure I could keep my eyes open much longer. "I'm going to bed," I stated. "And your glasses are crooked."

But I still couldn't sleep, this time wondering why love was so confusing, why I usually felt my very best with Jamie, but today, I didn't like how I'd acted right after Farah left—jealous, dishonest. I guess I'd assumed love equaled joy; I hadn't realized love might bring out the worst in you, too.

But none of that was Jamie's fault, or love's. I was responsible for my own actions. I was the one who called Farah's hair limp.

Hugging Big Muchli close, I closed my eyes and remembered how passionately we'd kissed in the van, how we'd played chopstick wars at the Amazing Chinese Restaurant and how it made me so happy to keep my foot against his leg the whole meal, how for once Jamie had done most of the talking. He told me how, when his father left them, Jamie had burned all of his photos, then swept up the remnants and stored them in his piggy bank because he felt guilty, how his father died in a motorcycle accident a few months later, how he still had the piggy bank with his father's photographic ashes.

Hearing this, I wanted to cross the table and embrace him, comfort that sad, sweet, guilty boy hidden inside, kiss his hurt away, assure him everything would be all right, that I was there for him, always.

I offered him a shrimp dumpling instead, except it fell from my chopsticks onto his lap.

Jamie said, "Missed connection," and even though I laughed, my heart ached a little. Because we'd talked about our fathers but we still hadn't talked about *us*, and we were running out of time.

Seventeen

THE NEXT DAY, I texted Farah to ask what she thought of Jamie.

Seems nice, she responded.

I called her immediately. "Nice? That's the worst. Did you not like him?"

"I like him fine," she said.

She was a terrible liar.

"You're a terrible liar," I told her.

She sighed. "I didn't not like him. And shouldn't we talk about what matters more?"

"What do you mean?"

"Why are you in love with him?"

"Because he's cute," I said.

"Okay. That'll only take you so far, though. What else?"

I groaned impatiently. This was classic Farah, to avoid answering by interrogating me instead. "Because he listens," I replied. "Because he's nice to me, because he likes me."

"So you love him because he's cute and because he likes you."

"You say that like it's bad."

"Shouldn't you love him because of his character? Because he's empathetic, intelligent, kind—I don't know, quirky, witty, sentimental?"

"Of course I love his character! He's really fast, and graceful. And adventurous. And usually fidgeting annoys me, but when he does it it's sexy."

"All I'm saying is that you say you love him, but how well do you really know him?"

"I know him," I said. "God, Farah, why do you have to think so deeply about everything? Love is a feeling. It's almost like . . . instinct. There's a reason that in Urdu poetry they say the liver is the seat of passion, not the brain. One day, when you actually fall in love, you'll know what I mean."

Farah was silent. I braced myself for further argument, but she said, "Please. I'm going to be a crazy old lady who grows a beard and lives with twenty cats."

"You hate cats."

"I won't after I grow a beard."

"You're going to meet someone awesome," I assured her. "Who'll love you and your beard."

Farah let out one of her gravely, raucous laughs. Every time I heard her laugh this way, my happiness quotient went up ten degrees.

"Just be careful, okay?" she said, suddenly sober. "The heart is a precious thing."

It was a precious thing, and I was determined to offer it—vulnerable, ecstatic, madly whirling—to Jamie. As soon as he told me he liked me.

There were nine days left for him to say it.

And then there were eight.

Then seven.

Seven was nothing. Seven was one week.

But I'd mapped it out; I would use some of my work/study money to visit Jamie in Madison over fall break, and he would come visit me, we would see each other once a month, and maybe next summer I could stay in Philly and he could be there, too. It was doable. All I needed was for him to agree, to say he liked me enough to not let this end.

There were moments when I believed the words were imminent; like now, in the half-lit shack after a heavy hookup session, our bodies equally sweaty for once, his arms wrapped around me, my back against his chest, my head resting on the slope of his shoulder.

I reached up to touch his cheek, and when he looked down at me he said, "Your eyes are shining."

Because you lit the lamp of my heart, I thought, but was

too shy to say, so I willed him to say it instead. I held his gaze, smiled, hoped, waited.

"What are you thinking, Morning Dew?" Jamie asked.

Tell him, I thought. What do you have to lose?

My pride, for one. And that thing we call a heart.

"Nothing much," I said. "You?"

"I'm thinking about how nice it is to be here with you," he said. "I am also thinking about those amazing donuts. Should we go get one once you're done with work?"

"Sure," I said.

"Great. Text me when you're done and I'll pick you up," he said. "Should we ask your friend Farah?"

"I think she's busy," I said.

"Cool," he said, and I was relieved he let it go. I was glad Farah had finally met him, but I wasn't about to share any more of our dwindling time with her, or anyone.

Eighteen

"SHABNAM! JUST THE PERSON I was hoping to see!" Dino cried when we walked into Ye Olde. By now, I'd heard Dino say this line many times to many customers, but I also knew he always meant it. Even if the donuts weren't so delicious, Dino's effusive embrace of the world and all its varied inhabitants would have kept people coming.

Dino smiled at Jamie. "You've brought a new friend."

"This is Jamie," I said.

Dino nodded, but before he could greet Jamie properly, more customers came in, so we placed our order and moved on.

On the way to the jukebox to queue up some Radiohead. I passed the old Bosnian men, only three today, drinking coffee in small ceramic cups and playing cards. I knew they were less than thrilled about my approach, because they preferred Bosnian music or Frank Sinatra, but, as Dino's regulars, we'd grown to tolerate each other's musical tastes. The one with eyebrows bushier than my father's even half smiled at me.

"This place is like a cross between the *Jetsons* and *Casablanca*," Jamie said as I slid onto the bench. "How do you not spend every day here?"

"I think there was one week where I did come here every day," I said.

"Please, come every day," Dino said, standing over us. His T-shirt displayed the golden eagle and blue crest of his favorite soccer team, Manchester City.

"Did your team win?" I asked.

He kissed his fingertips. "Did they win? But without Džeko, it's not the same."

Dino glanced back at the register and sat down next to Jamie. He was starting to gray at the temples. You could tell, though, that he was one of those men who'd still be handsome at seventy.

"Who's Džeko?" Jamie asked.

"Best Bosnian football player alive," Dino replied.

"You're from Bosnia?" Jamie said.

"Yes," he replied.

"You're so friendly, for an Eastern European," Jamie said.

I was worried Dino would be offended, but he chuckled. "And you? Where are you from?"

"Wisconsin," Jamie answered. "America's dairy land.

Everyone's friendly there."

"Wisconsin. Very nice. You're in school?" Dino asked.

"Yeah, at U. Wisconsin Madison."

"You get good grades?"

"Uh . . . sort of," Jamie said, slightly abashed.

"You like football?"

"Football like soccer? Not really."

"What car do you drive?"

"Right now, an old Dodge minivan. She's a beauty."

"Good shocks?"

"Replaced them last summer."

Dino nodded approvingly. "What are you studying at school?"

"I'm still undecided," Jamie replied.

"You have time," Dino said. "But not too much time."

It was cute to see Dino turn all paternal and give my date the third degree, something my own father would never do.

"Did you always want to be a donut maker, Dino?" I asked.

"No, no. I wanted to be a football player, once upon a time," Dino replied. "It was my dream. I wasn't very good, but I had very stubborn ambition. Then, one day, my coach came to me and said, 'Maybe you should switch to the javelin throw.'"

"Ouch," Jamie said, and we laughed.

"It broke my heart, but he was right—I became a javelin throw champion!" Dino proclaimed.

"A man of many talents," I said. "By the way, Jamie's a baker, too."

"Oh?" Dino said.

"I help my aunt bake pies for Andromeda's Pie Shack," Jamie explained.

"Ah, yes, the pie shack," Dino said. "I've had those pies—excellent. The crust is so flaky, so light!"

"I still haven't tried one," I confessed.

"What?" Jamie exclaimed. "How can that be?"

"I always mean to save one but there's usually a line and I feel bad keeping one. I mean, the people in line are so *excited*."

"As they should be," Jamie remarked.

"So what's the secret to your dough?" Dino inquired.

"Aunt Marianne would say it's because we sing as we're rolling it," Jamie said.

Dino nodded. "I sometimes talk to the donuts when they're done frying."

"What do you say?" I asked.

"I ask, what would you like to be? Blueberry, chocolate cream, vanilla? If it's morning, I say, Good morning!"

We all laughed.

"What time do you start your baking?" Jamie asked Dino. "My aunt and I start at five."

"Four, usually."

"Wow, that is really early," I said.

"There's a saying in Bosnia," Dino replied. "The man who gets up early is double lucky."

"So did you come here as genocide refugee?" Jamie asked him.

I had no idea where that question came from, and I couldn't believe how casually Jamie had said it. Meanwhile, Dino's perpetual smile had vanished.

"Yes," Dino said. "I did."

"Cool," Jaime said.

Cool?

"I read somewhere that they're still digging up mass graves the size of soccer—football—fields," Jamie said. "And that they had concentration camps. What was it like for you?"

I had to intervene. "Dino needs to work," I said.

"It's all right, Shabnam," Dino assured me. "Jamie isn't the first one to ask me about this." He folded his hands on the table and sat up very straight, as if what he was about to say demanded proper posture. "During the siege of Sarajevo, the Serbs cut off our supply of everything—water, food, fuel. The winters are cold there, we needed fire to stay warm, to cook food. We used what we could for fuel, wood floors, old shoes, chairs, and books, lots of books. We had no choice, it was either freeze and starve, or burn our books. We'd look at our books and think, which ones should we burn today? When I moved here, I went to many used bookstores, I bought many books, even ones I knew I wouldn't read. I put up a wall of books in my house, a wall of books in this shop. I like to look at them and know I will never have to burn any of them, I will never have to choose."

"Wow," Jamie said. "That's fascinating. Did you know Shabnam's uncle is also a genocide survivor?"

For Chrissake.

"Oh?" Dino said. I didn't like seeing him so serious.

"He was the lone survivor of this crazy train massacre," Jamie continued. "Tell him, Morning Dew."

"I don't feel like talking about it right now," I said.

"Don't worry," Dino said. "No need to tell. I'm sure every genocide is different, and every genocide is the same."

He stood up, and I was relieved by the return of his trademark broad smile.

"Time to make the donuts," he said. "Very good to meet you, Jamie. Please come again soon."

"For sure," Jamie said.

If Dino had been offended, he was too kind to show it.

"Damn, they had to burn books," Jamie said. "You ever read *Fahrenheit 451*? They memorized—"

"Jamie, can we get out of here?"

"What's up? You okay?"

I shook my head.

"All right, but I have to hit the restroom. Meet you outside?"

I paced the parking lot, becoming more furious with each step. I wished I could call Farah and bitch about what Jamie had said, but I didn't want her thinking badly of him.

When Jamie came out I led him behind the shop, where the Dumpsters were. "What the hell was that?" I cried.

"What the hell was what?" Jamie replied.

"Why did you ask Dino about the Bosnian genocide?"

Jamie pushed back his hair, his brow knitting together. "I was curious. He didn't seem upset by it—why are you?"

"Just because he didn't say anything doesn't mean he wasn't upset! Maybe people who've lived through a genocide don't want to talk about it! Would you go up to some old Jewish lady at a bagel shop and be like, 'Hey, how was the Holocaust for you?'"

"Maybe sometimes people do want to talk about it. It's nothing to be ashamed of, right? Didn't your uncle talk to you about it?" Jamie pointed out.

If I'd understood how long the life span of my Partition lie would be, how it would keep flaring up again like a case of herpes, I would never have told it.

"My *great*-uncle. And that's another thing—why did you have to bring him up?"

"I figured Dino would be interested, since they have something in common."

"Something in common? It's not like they're both fond of horse racing, or . . . pedigree poodles! And maybe I wanted to keep that story about my great-uncle private."

"Oh," Jamie said. "I'm sorry. I didn't know."

"Obviously!" Seeing Jamie penitent was dampening my fury, but something else was bothering me.

"MD? What is it?"

"I don't know." But as soon as I said this, I realized what it was; the way Jamie had brought up my great-uncle, like, here's an interesting tidbit about Shabnam. It was that a lot of what he found interesting about me wasn't really me, or at least, not all of me. Not even close.

I took a deep breath. "I feel like the things that interest you about me are Partition and biryani and Urdu poetry! Which is really ironic because I didn't live through Partition, and I can't cook biryani, and as of a month ago I knew jack about Urdu poetry! Sometimes I don't know if . . . if you even see *me*."

Jamie started making shushing sounds, cupping my sniffing face in his hands.

"Look at me," he said. "I'm standing right here in front of you, and I see you. I see you, Morning Dew."

Somewhere between the first "see" and the second, I'd started crying.

"Hey, hey." Jamie wiped my tears with his thumbs, kissed the top of my head. "Don't cry, my beautiful girl. Don't ever cry."

He called me his girl. It was the first time he'd ever claimed me. My sad tears turned happy.

Funny, how everything could turn on a pronoun.

"How about this," Jamie said, rubbing my back. "Aunt Marianne's gone to the city tonight, and you're a pie wallah who hasn't tried the pie. Why don't you come over to her house and I'll bake you one?"

A house. A house meant couches. A house meant beds. A house meant space to roll around.

A house was incredibly exciting and utterly terrifying.

One week left.

"I would love that," I said.

Nineteen

"BRACE YOURSELF," JAMIE SAID as he opened the front door, though nothing could have prepared me for the dramatic entrance into Aunt Marianne's house. Hundreds of African masks decorated both walls of the long, high-ceilinged entry hall, their expressions covering the range of human emotion, from joy to rage to sorrow to grief.

I paused in front of an entire floor-to-ceiling section of giraffe masks.

"Aunt Marianne's favorite animal," Jamie explained.

"Did I take a wrong turn and end up backstage at *The Lion King*?" I said.

Jamie laughed. "Come," he said.

I followed him to the hallway's end. Ahead was a wooden

staircase, a lovely deep red Persian carpet running down it; to the right, a bathroom; to the left, a sleek, massive kitchen that could have been featured in a modern design magazine—marble counters; a large, butcher-block table in the center; gleaming stainless steel appliances, including a double oven; and, most notably after all those masks, not a single decorative item, not even a magnet on the fridge.

"So this is where the magic happens," I said.

"You got it," he replied. "I'll get the dough—go check out the living room."

Three broad steps led from the kitchen to the sunken living room, its visual cacophony echoing that of the hallway, except this room spanned the globe instead of one continent—a marble replica of the Taj Mahal, Indian miniatures in wrought silver frames, bamboo flutes and Peruvian blankets, bronze Buddha statues and more Persian rugs and Chinese landscape paintings and bright tapestries woven with geometric designs, Mexican tiled tables.

"What do you think of the house?" Jamie called out from the kitchen.

"Stupendous," I said.

"Stupendous," Jamie repeated. "That's a good word."

The living room's enormous windows looked onto an expansive, slightly wild backyard, where a pair of bluebirds fed at an umbrella-shaped feeder. Bordering the backyard was forest so thick that you'd never guess you were in suburban New Jersey, that the mall was only fifteen minutes away, the turnpike even closer.

"Has she been to all these places?" I asked.

"Some. A lot are gifts from her ex-lovers."

She must have slept with half the UN, I thought.

I examined a bronze ewer on the bookshelf. It looked ancient, like if I rubbed it thrice, a jinni might actually appear. What would my three wishes be? Jamie and I, together, in love. A million dollars. My parents, happy. Farah and I, 100 percent cool again.

That was four.

Jamie touched my shoulder, and I jumped. "Sorry, didn't mean to startle you. The dough has to warm up a bit. Should we have some wine?"

Wine. The only alcoholic beverages I'd ever consumed were crappy beer and Jell-O shots. Wine was high-class, luxurious.

Like Dom Perignon. I'd forgotten I'd tried that, too.

"I'd love some," I said, trying not to sound too eager.

He squatted in front of the barrel wine rack in the corner. "Hmmmm. How about a Malbec?"

I had no idea what Malbec was. "Perfect," I said.

Jamie sprinted to the kitchen, returned with two glasses, and proceeded to open the bottle with the Swiss Army knife in his back pocket. It was sexy to watch him maneuver the cork out, almost as sexy as watching him drive stick shift. If we were stranded somewhere, in the heat of the Sahara, in the midst of dense jungle, Jamie would surely know what to do.

I could follow him anywhere.

"Let's drink out on the deck," he said.

We sipped wine outside, listening to the rustle of leaves and a choir of birds. As I relaxed into the setting and my beverage, I regretted having been so upset at Jamie. Sure, he'd been a little inappropriate, but he had meant well. He was still good and kind, and I still loved him.

I decided Malbec was my favorite drink.

"How far back do those woods go?" I asked.

"Not too far. It's a small state park. I run the trails sometimes. There's a nice old oak I like to climb, gives you a great view of the reservoir."

"I've never climbed a tree," I confessed.

"What? Oh, right—you're scared of heights."

I doubted I'd have climbed one even if I weren't.

"We should climb a tree one day."

I was tempted to ask for an exact date, like maybe the Saturday of Penn's fall break.

Jamie nudged my foot, and I nudged his back.

"I should go check on the dough," he said.

We went back inside and he grabbed his phone. "Any music preference?" he said. "Radiohead?"

"You choose," I told him.

"Shuffle," he declared.

A minute later, a man's deep, raspy voice filled the room, the sound so crisp and clean I sat up on the leather sofa and blurted, "Wow!"

"The whole house is wired with Bose speakers. Aunt Marianne once dated a sound engineer," Jamie explained.

Aunt Marianne's lovers had clearly served her well.

"Who is this?"

"Howlin' Wolf. Famous blues musician."

As Howlin' Wolf sang *shake it baby, shake it for me*, Jamie did a hip shake all the way to the kitchen. I followed him up the stairs, not daring to mimic an act so good, and observed as Jamie tested the dough, then sprinkled flour across the butcher-block table and set the ball of dough on top, dancing the entire time.

Forget stick-shift-driving Jamie; lithe, graceful-dancing Jamie was the sexiest of them all. Emboldened by wine, I started dancing across the table from him.

When the song ended, Jamie exclaimed "Woo!" with a wide grin. The next song was a classical piano piece, wistful, slow.

Jamie bowed. "Would milady like to roll the dough?"

"I don't know how."

"Come. I'll show you."

I finished my remaining wine in one go and went to him. As he rolled up the sleeves of his plaid shirt, I admired his forearms, their sinewy muscle, how his hair started out darker at his wrists and slowly faded to gold.

"Now, the first thing Aunt Marianne makes me do is clear my mind and think positive thoughts, because dough that's shaped by happy hands will taste better. Ready?"

"Ready."

Jamie closed his eyes, so I closed mine. Positive thoughts.

I love you I love you I love you

I felt so loose and good I actually sighed audibly. Wine was like a sultry muscle relaxant.

Sultry. Another good word.

"Someone's smiling," Jamie said.

I opened my eyes, and he gave me a quick kiss.

"So you start by moving from the center out, like this," he instructed, flattening and widening the dough with the rolling pin. "You have to make sure you're applying even pressure, and keep the dough in the shape of a circle. Each stroke should be the same distance apart from the last, about this much. Aunt Marianne likes to rotate the dough to control the distance, but I prefer to move the pin—like this. Here, you try."

My first few rolls succeeded in completely destroying the lovely circle Jamie had created. "Oops."

"Let me help." He moved behind me, placed his hands over mine on the handles of the rolling pin. As he skillfully reshaped the dough into a circle, each stroke a quarter turn or so off from the last, his body pressed closer and closer into me, until I felt him grow hard against the small of my back.

"Shit," he said. "I'm getting an erection just standing next to you."

He let go of the rolling pin and spun me around. Grabbing my waist, he hoisted me onto the counter as though I weighed nothing, and we started wildly making out. When his hand crawled up my shirt, I arched my back, urging him onward, and as his thumb slid beneath my bra, along the underside of my breasts, I made a noise I didn't even know I was capable of, an animal-like utterance. Jamie leaned back and I could see the excitement in his eyes. He reached behind me, undid my bra with one hand and bent down, sliding his tongue where his thumb had just been.

I gasped, clutching at his lovely hair, and then I noticed the song playing.

Everyone stop trying to put a label on me

Everyone stop trying to put a label on me

Jamie lifted his head. "What's the matter?" he asked.

I shook my head, unsure of myself. "This is the band Farah likes."

"Yeah, Rebel Antigone. I downloaded their album. *I'm not a girl I'm not a guy I'm not an x I'm not a y*," Jamie sang along, stroking my cheek. "You sure you're okay, Morning Dew?"

Why should I be bothered by the fact he'd downloaded a song?

"Yeah." To prove it, I kissed him, trying to return to where we were. But I couldn't re-create the past, because nothing can be the same as it was even a moment ago. The now was always changing, and now it was dark out, and I'd told my mother I'd be home by eight.

On cue, my phone rang.

"It's my mother," I said. "I better go."

As I slid off the table, I saw the dough now bore an indentation from my butt. Whoops.

He tugged at a curl. "I wish we could have at least one time where we wouldn't be interrupted by people waiting for pies, or a phone."

"We can," I said, smacking bits of dough off my ass. "What about tomorrow night? My parents are going to a party, I could probably stay out till eleven."

"I'm meeting a friend in New York this weekend. What about Monday?"

"Monday night? Sure," I said, already trying to think of what my excuse would be.

He kissed me. "I had a great time. You sure you're not still upset about what I said to Dino?"

"No." I couldn't stay mad at him anyway. One hip shake and the rest was history.

Twenty

I TEXTED FARAH.

U free to come over this wknd? Need advice.

4 what?

Ill tell you when I cu!

Don't think i can, my khalas in town

please please

She didn't respond, so Sunday morning I tried again.

Please? It's really impt . . .

Ok, persistent. lemme c what I can do

I was used to Farah's dramatic outfits, but when she came to our house Sunday afternoon, even I did a double take. She was wearing a green-and-black-checkered scarf, the bottom part wrapped right around her head, the rest of it a braided roll that went from the top of her head down—a hijab Mohawk. Her long black skirt looked like it was made from pieces of shredded cloth, and she was wearing leather cuffs over her sleeves, one with a silver skull and one with a peace sign.

"Salaam, Auntie!" Farah exclaimed, hugging my mother as though she was a long-lost relative.

"So good to see you, *beti*! It's been too long! Look at your hijab!" My mother touched Farah's cheek. "I'm so proud of you, getting into Harvard, wearing hijab in a time when so many people hate Muslims."

Farah patted her Mohawk. "Tell that to my mother. She says I'm making a mockery of hijab, and threatened to disown me if I left the house like this."

"Oh, it's always hard for the old generation to accept the young fashions," my mother said. "I remember when I first crimped my hair, my mother didn't want me to leave the house either. She said I looked like I was wearing a wig made of a swallow's nest."

"You crimped your hair?" I said.

"Yes, when I worked at Merry-Go-Round. Do you girls want some chai? Snacks?" my mother offered.

Before Farah could answer in the affirmative, I said, "Farah and I have important stuff to do."

"All right," my mother said, clearly disappointed.

"Your mom is so cool," Farah said. "Where's her weirdo half? I want to say salaams."

As we walked into the den, Farah glanced at the bookshelf that housed my mother's horrible tchotchkes, the four dumb white cherubs watching from high. I'd never told Farah about my recent theory that they represented the children my mother almost had. Farah would never joke about something like that, cheesy as it was, but it still didn't feel right to reveal the contents of my mother's hidden trauma chest.

My father was watching BBC News, a bowl of masala popcorn resting on his tummy, a trail of kernels from chin to couch.

"Salaam, Uncle Q!" Farah cried, plunking herself down on the armchair.

"What happened to your head?" my father said. "You look like you're from outer space."

"I was on a mission to Pluto," Farah replied. "We went to tell him in person that he's no longer a planet. We thought it was the considerate thing to do. He took it pretty hard, poor dwarf bastard."

My father blinked a few times, speechless. Witnessing my father and Farah interact was extremely entertaining, because she was unfazed by his eccentricity and he was bewildered by hers.

"She's kidding," I said.

"Obviously," my father said. "A mission to Pluto would take twenty years round-trip."

"So, I hear you've been teaching Shabnam the language of love?" Farah said, leaning forward and helping herself to popcorn. While I had to think before saying a sentence in Urdu, her Urdu was fluent, with barely an accent, her genders always correct; and while with my mother she used mainly English, with my father she switched back and forth seamlessly, like he did.

"Which language are you referring to?" my father asked, and I could tell Farah was trying hard not to laugh.

"The language of love, also known in some circles as Urdu poetry," she explained. "Will you teach me a little? Like the moth and the flame—what's that all about?"

"Ah." My father set the popcorn aside, sat up, wiped the top of his head with a napkin. Even the slightest spice caused my father's scalp to break out in sweat.

"The moth and the flame is a trope of Urdu poetry," he told Farah. "The moth is the lover, the flame the beloved. The moth is so in love with the flame that he keeps circling it, getting closer and closer, until he decides even being this close is not sufficient, so he flies into the flame and burns himself alive, and, by dying in this way, finally becomes one with his beloved."

"So basically it's emotional torture for the moth until he burns himself up," Farah said. "Like, life sucks *until* you die."

"Come on," I said, grabbing Farah's hand. "Let's go upstairs."

"*Khuda hafiz*, Uncle Q," Farah said, scooping a fistful of popcorn. "What does your mother put in this?" she asked. "It's good."

"Some chili powder, a little garam masala, I think. Don't spill any, I'm on vacuum duty all summer and if my mother sees one kernel she'll hand me the Hoover."

When we entered my room, Farah went straight for Big Muchli. "Did you miss me?" she asked him, planting a loud smooch on his worn snout.

"How long did it take you to do the Mohawk?"

"Don't ask," she said. "I mostly did it to piss my mother off. Yesterday she told me I was 'giving Islam bad name' because I looked like a homeless trash can, but it's starting to grow on me."

"What the hell is a homeless trash can?"

"Me, apparently."

"What if she really does disown you?" I asked.

"She won't," Farah assured me. "I'm her retirement plan."

It was a lot of pressure, to know you'd have to help take care of your parents and your three younger siblings, but Farah never acted bitter about it, only determined.

"Anyway, what was so important that I had to escape my visiting relatives?" she said.

"I need outfit advice from the homeless trash can."

"*Outfit* advice?"

"I have a hot date with Jamie."

"Ah. Where is he taking you? Fancy dinner?"

"I don't know, it's a surprise," I said. "And listen—I'm using you as an excuse."

"For real, Qureshi? You know I'm a terrible liar."

"I told my mother I'm taking you for dinner and a movie as an early birthday present."

"My birthday's in October."

"Exactly, and you'll be at Harvard, and I'll be at Penn. It scored me an eleven p.m. curfew."

"And what if she calls me?" Farah demanded.

"Tell her I'm with you."

"And what if she asks to talk to you?"

"Tell her I'm on my way home."

Farah groaned.

"It'll be fine," I insisted.

"What if your mother calls my mother?"

"She wouldn't call your mother unless I didn't come home at all. I'll be home by eleven p.m. sharp. She won't even have to call you, I promise."

"You could have at least asked me," Farah objected.

"Sorry. Come on, help me out. It's the night of union with my beloved."

"Fine," she conceded. "But if this blows up—"

"Nothing's going to blow up," I vowed.

"Insert bad Muslim joke here," she said. "What kind of outfit are you thinking?"

"I want to look sexy. And sultry. But I also don't want to look like I'm trying too hard, you know? Basically, I want him to look at me and never want to let me go."

"You're asking the hijabi for advice on sexy and sultry?"

"Who else? Danny? Ian?"

"Uh, hello—queer eye for the straight girl or homeless trash can?"

"Homeless trash can!" I replied, and Farah shook her head. "Anyway, Danny and Ian are still on their road trip, plus I sent them photos of three outfit options and they negged all of them. I want you to look at my top two. I'm also going to go to Victoria's Secret to buy some hot underwear. I think I might go all the way."

Farah frowned. "With Jamie?"

"No, with Principal Stone. Of course with Jamie. Why?"

Farah's hand disappeared inside the shreds of her skirts into what must have been a pocket, because it emerged with a black marker.

"All right, what is it?" I said as she began drawing on her foot. "If you don't tell me in two seconds, I'm taking the marker away. I mean it."

"I know you love him," she said, "but has he said he loves you?"

"No. Not yet."

"But you're still willing to have sex with him?"

"You really don't like him at all, do you?" I exclaimed.

"I'm looking out for you. You're totally moth and flaming this shit, and forget about love, this guy hasn't even told you he wants to keep seeing you after he leaves. And isn't he leaving this week?"

"Maybe he's waiting for Monday," I pointed out. "Maybe that's why he planned a big surprise. That's why I need to look good."

"If he really loves you, it shouldn't matter what you're wearing," Farah argued. "And what if he doesn't tell you? What if this isn't the same for him as it is for you? Maybe you should stop being so passive and ask him how he actually feels about you before you let him stick his penis in your vagina."

"You just don't approve of me having sex," I countered.

"It's not your hymen I'm concerned about," she said. "It's your heart."

"You're saying that like you're assuming he doesn't have good intentions. You have no idea how caring and thoughtful he is with me. By the way, he thought you were great, including your musical taste. You really shouldn't judge him when you hardly know him."

"You're right, I hardly know him," Farah said. "And you've known him for what, a few weeks?"

"In Bollywood it takes one song to fall in love." I was joking, of course. Sort of.

"Come on, Qureshi. You're smarter than this."

"You come on! It's so easy for you to stand there on the other side and judge but you have no clue what it's like to date someone, to like someone, to kiss and cuddle with someone! But me, I'm in it. I am in the thick of the garden. I am making myself totally vulnerable—I don't think you'd ever even let yourself be as vulnerable as I am right now, but that's what love is all about, Farah. Being the nightingale. Offering your heart to the rose."

"Nightingale? Your father has created an Urdu poetry monster." She was joking. Sort of.

"I *love* him, Farah," I declared, quivering lip and all. "I really do. Please, will you be there for me?"

Farah held her hands up, an unfinished game of tic-tac-toe on her foot. "All right, Ms. Nightingale. I hope this rose is worthy of your love. Show me what you were thinking of wearing."

As I started laying out my outfit options, I got a text from Jamie.

Wear clothes you don't mind getting dirty 4 2morrow, like hiking clothes

I didn't even own hiking clothes.

Track pants and sneakers ok?

Yup

Where are we going?

I could tell u but I'd have to kill u . . . ☺

"Well," I said, showing Farah the exchange, "I guess that settles the outfit question."

"He's taking you on a hike?"

"He's really outdoorsy." I would have preferred a romantic dinner, but a hike could be romantic, too, kissing in moonlight, staring up at the stars. Hopefully he'd bring some more Malbec.

"I gotta go," Farah said. "Good luck tomorrow."

She had this uncomfortable, mouth ajar expression, like her

throat was gargling whatever words she'd left unsaid. I didn't press her; I wanted to focus on my big night, surround myself with positivity. I loved Farah but she could be a real drag when it came to romance. I hoped her parents' toxic relationship hadn't jaded her for life.

Farah had hardly been gone five minutes when there was a knock on my door. My mother, of course; my father never came to my room, but my mother came by almost every night, though she found it difficult to tolerate the mess. I'd explained to her that there was order in my disorder, and she knew better than to touch anything, but it took all of her self-control not to pick up a sock from the floor, or fold the shirts thrown over my chair, or return a book to the shelf. During times of extreme disorder, she sometimes had to sit on her hands.

At least, unlike my father, I was *clean* messy; no food detritus, all dirty clothes in the hamper, no spiderwebs or ants.

"Farah left so soon. She didn't want to stay over?" my mother said. She was dressed in a billowing lavender muumuu and a blue shower cap; she'd put henna in her hair.

"She has relatives visiting."

"Everything okay between you two?"

"Everything's great."

"Are you sure?"

"Yes, I'm sure."

"And everything else is okay?"

"Everything's great, Mom."

She made her way to my bed, sitting next to the jeans and lace-trimmed black T-shirt I'd set out as a potential outfit for tomorrow night.

I remembered my mother telling me once that any boy who respected a girl would never touch her. How would she ever understand that I wanted to be touched? That I loved Jamie?

She hadn't even held hands with my father before she married him.

Had she ever had an orgasm with Dad?

Gross.

"Why are you making that face?" my mother asked.

There was an orange streak across her forehead from the henna. Tomorrow, when the sun hit her hair, you'd see sparks of red.

"Can I ask you something?" I said.

"Of course."

"Of the proposals you received, why did you choose Dad?"

My mother picked up Big Muchli, gently stroking his back. "He was different."

"Please elaborate."

"Well, everyone else came to our house with their mother, or their *khala*. Your father came alone. Back then, he had a full head of curly hair, and these square-shaped glasses, they kept sliding down his nose. All the other ones were doctor, engineer, doctor, engineer. They said boring things. Your father was a mathematician, and he said funny things. He felt like a breath of fresh air.

I remember my father asked him, 'What are your intentions for the future?' And your father said, 'I'm afraid, given the vastness of the universe, my intentions for the future will have zero impact on what the future will actually be.'"

I laughed. "God. That is so Dad."

"I know. My father didn't know what to say, and I giggled behind my hands. And after he came to our house, he sent me a verse."

"He wrote you a verse?" I said.

"Yes. I'd been wearing jasmine perfume, and I can't remember all of it, but one line was, I guess you'd translate it, *the scent of your jasmine has stirred new life into the desert of my heart*."

"Dad noticed your perfume?" I said.

"He did."

"False advertising," I joked, and she chuckled.

It was funny, but it was also her life, a husband who wouldn't remember her birthday if I didn't remind him every year. "Is that why jasmine is your favorite perfume?"

"Yes," my mother said, with this sweet, bashful smile that suddenly made her seem crimped-hair young.

"But he's . . . so in his own world. It's not fair to you," I said.

"What is fair, Shabu?" she said. "Every day I try to help women who have so little, who were abused by their husbands, who are struggling to make a good life for their children. No one has a perfect life, but I have a dear husband, and you, my sweet miracle. Your father and I have good jobs, a good house."

Sometimes I wasn't sure if my mother was more saintly or delusional. Her dear husband never did the dishes, never said thank you. Her sweet miracle led a double life.

At the very least, my mother deserved a more considerate partner.

"Dad loves you," I said. "He told me himself, the other day."

"He said that?"

"Yup."

"I thought you only talked about poetry."

"Sometimes we talk about other things."

"What things?" she asked.

"I don't know, the weather, donuts. Listen, should we see a movie next weekend?" I offered.

"Yes, please," my mother said, her face aglow. It took so little to please my mother that I almost felt embarrassed, like she should demand more in exchange for happiness. Except, given the nature of her family, that would only cause further disappointment.

But if my father had once written a verse for my mother, surely he could do so again.

Twenty-One

"WHAT HAPPENED HERE?" I asked Jamie, gently touching the fresh cut on his hand. It intersected at an angle with his scar, forming a teepee shape above his wrist.

"I was removing glass from a window."

"Does it hurt?"

"As a wise man once said, pain is inevitable, suffering is optional. Shit—that's our exit. Hold on, MD," he said as he swiftly crossed over three lanes, smoothly decelerating onto the exit ramp.

The exit was for the town of Merritt. I didn't know anything about it except that it was home to Merritt College, a small liberal arts college.

"When are you going to tell me where we're going? And why

were you removing glass from a window?"

"Patience, young Jedi," he replied, turning right after a blue sign that read *Merritt College est. 1894*. He parked on the street, grabbed his khaki rucksack from the backseat, and came around to open my door, offering me his wounded hand.

"Come," he said.

We entered campus, following a path that led to a leafy green quadrangle surrounded by an eclectic mix of architectural styles: ivy-covered brick, domed Grecian temple, modern steel and glass.

"Have you been here before?" I spoke very quietly, even though there was no one in sight.

"I came last year," Jamie said. "To see a Mongolian throat-singing performance with Aunt Marianne."

As we walked past the windowless, cubic engineering building, Jamie pulled me behind a long hedge.

"What's going on?" I whispered.

The headlights of a campus security golf cart cutting through the quadrangle were my answer.

"Jamie—"

"Don't worry. We're almost there."

We took a right after the engineering cube, following another path that led us away from the quad, past an art studio building and algae-covered pond, ending in front of a gothic-style building with pointed windows, arched doorways, a steep roof, and a tall parapet. It was massive and foreboding, an Edgar Allan Poe poem come to life. Ivy crawled up its gray stone walls, and the doors and the first floor windows were boarded up. The cornerstone read *RAVENWOOD HALL 1925.*

"What do you think of her?" Jamie asked.

As I craned my neck to the top of the parapet, the pale yellow moon, half full, emerged from behind a cloud. "She's beautiful."

"I first saw her last year when we came for the concert. Took my breath away—I had to come back and break in and meet her. They apparently boarded her up sometime in the nineties."

"You mean you've been inside?"

With a grin, Jamie bent down and started running along the side of the building. I mimicked his actions, my heart racing from adrenaline and fear. This was crazy. We were daredevils, trespassers, spies on a reconnaissance mission. Behind the building was a fancy black metal fence; behind that, dark woods. The grass had been left untended, stringy weeds brushing against my calves.

"Why don't they restore Ravenwood Hall?" I said. "Are they just going to let her fall apart?"

"Probably costs too much money to bring it up to code. They'll have to do something one day, either fix her up or tear her down."

Poor Ravenwood Hall, shuttered and lonely and in limbo.

Jamie put on a headlamp. Its light exposed bits of brick and glass, crushed cigarette packs and candy wrappers caught in the overgrowth. Right at my foot was a torn condom wrapper.

"Should we say hello?" he said.

"But how will we get inside?"

He shone his light on a first floor window that had been freed of boards and glass.

I gasped. "Is that how you got your cut?"

"Yeah, I wanted to make sure we had easy access. Was here by three a.m., back to the house at four in time to bake."

"Did you even sleep last night?"

"Barely. Ready to go in?"

I swallowed. "I think so."

"Seize the time, Meribor. Now will never come again," he said.

"What?"

"You can do this, Morning Dew. It's easy."

But the bottom of the window was level with my chin. "How will we get up there?"

"You see that?" Jamie pointed to a carved stone pipe sticking out of the building. "Put your foot on it, and you can hoist yourself up. I'll help you."

Jamie offered me his hand, and I made a brave face. If he thought I could do it, I didn't want to disappoint him. With Jamie guiding me, I placed my foot on the pipe and managed to hoist myself up, though at one point Jamie had to assist, giving me a boost through the window.

Inside, it was so dark I didn't dare move until Jamie entered, jumping down from the windowsill with the grace of a cat burglar. He turned his head in both directions to illuminate the room, the chalkboard on the wall, the tall stacks of desks and chairs covered with stained sheets, cobwebs stretching from one sheet to the next.

"This way," Jamie said, heading for the door.

"What's out there?" I asked.

"Classrooms and offices, some empty, some filled with furniture. There's a library on the third floor, and you can climb from there to the top of the tower, but the stairs are rotting a little. My foot went through one of the steps last time."

"How many times have you been in here?"

"This is my third."

Third time's the charm, I thought, as he opened the door with one hand and reached for mine with the other.

As we stepped into the hallway, something groaned. I clutched Jamie's arm.

"Creaky floorboard," he assured me, but I didn't ease my grip. It was nice to have an excuse to hold him so tight.

Beyond the light of the headlamp, the hall disappeared into an endless dark. The floor below was scattered with bits of paper and debris. We passed a display case, and Jamie paused to show me the old class photos inside, rows of young men in black coats and slicked-back hair. One photo had fallen to the bottom of the case; three young men in high-waisted shorts and white T-shirts smiled up at us, round medals hanging from their necks.

I heard a high-pitched screech.

"What was that?"

"Barn owl," Jamie said. "He lives up in the tower, I think."

We walked a few more steps, and Jamie announced, "We have arrived." He rotated his head to the right to reveal a vaulted ceiling, two sets of grand double doors. He pushed open one of these doors, saying, "After you, Morning Dew."

The room was carpeted, sloped. Rows and rows of red cushioned chairs led to what looked like a stage, with drawn curtains. "Is this a theater?" I asked.

"Affirmative," Jamie said.

As we walked toward the stage, I felt like we were being watched by an audience of ghosts who'd been suspended in a dark, timeless intermission. If there were ghosts, I thought, surely they'd be happy to have some entertainment.

We climbed the stairs to the stage and Jamie instructed me to wait, disappearing behind the velvet curtains. Without his light, I could barely see. I remained very still, listening to Jamie's movements, my heart pounding in the pitch black.

The curtains slowly opened, particles of dust invading my nostrils. The stage had been set, lit by a circle of red candles in small jars. Inside the circle were an unzipped sleeping bag, a Peruvian blanket, and two small silk pillows I recognized from Marianne's den, a bouquet of daisies resting on top.

The scene took my breath away.

Tell me is this even real

The curtains came to a halt. Jamie stepped out, switched off his lamp.

This was real.

"I swept the stage this morning," he said. "It's better now, but I hope you're not allergic to dust. I brought some allergy medicine, in case."

He'd even thought to bring allergy medicine. So practical, and so romantic. "I'm not."

"Good. Well, welcome to the Theater of Dreams, as I call it."

Jamie and I entered the candlelit circle, sitting across from each other on the blanket.

I picked up the daisies, smelled them. "Where are these from?"

"Our field," he answered, and it took me a second to realize he meant the field next to the shack. He set out speakers and his phone. Its screen read *No Service*, which prompted me to check my own. I didn't have service, either.

We couldn't contact anyone and no one knew where we were. I had to get out of here in a timely fashion, to make sure my mother didn't call Farah. She'd be pissed if she had to lie to her. Plus Farah was such a crappy liar.

"I made a Radiohead playlist in your honor. And I figured we'd be hungry, so I brought dinner," he said, laying out two peanut butter and jelly sandwiches, a pack of almonds, two apples, and M&M's. "I was thinking of picking up Indian, but I didn't have the time. Plus this is more portable."

"This is great," I said.

"Ah—last but not least." He pulled a bottle of wine out of his backpack. "A bottle of Malbec."

Malbec forever and ever.

He opened the wine with his Swiss Army knife, measuredly pouring it into two plastic cups. "Oh, by the way," he said as he handed me one, "I also brought a bucket and put it backstage, in case you need to relieve yourself."

I made a note not to drink too much, as there was no way I was going to pee into a bucket backstage where Jamie would be able to hear.

"Cheers," Jamie said, holding up his sandwich. "To Ravenwood Hall."

"To Ravenwood Hall."

We toasted with our PB&Js and took a bite.

Delicious. "What kind of jam is this?" I asked.

"Marianne's friend makes homemade blackberry preserves."

Blackberry, blackberry, blackberry. I remembered my father's first letter, how he said Plato believed that everything on earth was a mere shadow of its perfect form, which would mean this PB&J sandwich was a mere shadow of the perfect PB&J sandwich that existed elsewhere, except that couldn't be true, because what made the PB&J perfect was not only its taste but the fact that Jamie had made it, that we were eating it here, together, in this Theater of Dreams, before an audience of ghosts. It was the *experience* of the form that made it perfect.

I felt very profound. Love really suited me.

"I know PB&J doesn't hold a candle to biryani," he apologized.

"No! This PB&J is perfect," I insisted.

"Good." He'd already finished and moved on to the M&M's. As perfect as the PB&J was, I had too many butterflies to eat more than two bites. Wine, on the other hand, went well with butterflies.

I took a sip of Malbec. "Didn't you say you were arrested for trespassing? You think that would have scared you into not doing it again."

"Only once. I got off with community service. My stepdad was friends with the judge."

"You should be careful," I admonished.

"Oh, I'm a lot more careful now. What about you, Morning Dew? You ever been reckless?"

"Apart from this?" I shook my head. "Not really. Well, smoking pot in the mall parking lot was pretty reckless, I guess."

"Yeah. But that was some good ganja." He lay down on his side, propped up on his elbow. His shadow flickered on the back wall of the stage, long, lean, larger than life. "She's something else, your friend Farah."

"Yeah."

"Have you ever thought about wearing a scarf?" he asked.

"Me? No."

"How come?"

"Not all Muslim women wear the headscarf. And I don't even know if I would call myself Muslim. I don't really think about Islam that much."

"What about Sufism, Allah as the beloved? You seem pretty into that."

"That's mysticism. That's not what you hear when you attend the *masjid*—the mosque," I said. "I don't know if I believe in organized religion. My father definitely doesn't. My mother wants to go on Hajj. She has to go with a close male relative, except her father is dead and she has no sons, but she'll never go with my dad because she's worried that as soon as they got to Saudi Arabia he'd start running his mouth and be executed for blasphemy."

"What's Hajj?"

"The pilgrimage to Mecca every Muslim is supposed to do at least once," I explained.

"Oh, right. Has Farah done it?"

"Not yet."

"Will you?"

"I don't know." I lay down next to him, hoping this would prompt him to kiss me.

"Almost forgot—I made a Radiohead playlist," Jamie exclaimed, flipping onto his stomach. As he figured out the music, I finished the wine, thinking I'd never able to drink Malbec again without remembering him, this night, this place.

Radiohead's "Packt Like Sardines in a Crushd Tin Box" started to play, and Jamie kissed me at last, a kiss that started out soft and sweet and tender and became increasingly urgent, wanting, like the harder we kissed the better to quench the thirst of a hundred thousand waits, of all those long, lonely desert nights.

When "Let Down" started to play, Jamie paused to whisper, "Our song."

We were naked except for our underwear, Jamie's mouth on my breasts. The song slowed, then built to a crescendo, and when it hit its peak, I had goose bumps again, because Thom Yorke's voice seemed to encapsulate all of our longing and passion, and the music was inside us and around us, carrying us, holding us, stoking our fire.

The audience of ghosts rose from their seats, whirling in ecstasy to the soft slide of Jamie's lips, the desirous heat of his breath, his body moving against mine, the dance of the rose and the nightingale, the moth and the flame, the lover and the beloved, united at last.

I love you so much so much so much

"Morning Dew?" Jamie raised himself on his arms, looking down, his erection teasing my belly button. "Are you all right?"

The song was ending, and it had all been so wonderfully intense that I'd suddenly started crying.

"I'm . . ." What word could do justice to this experience? "Perfect."

I couldn't stop the tears. Jamie smiled, touched his forehead to mine, and embraced me.

"House of Cards" started to play.

We closed our eyes, let the haunting ballad wash over us.

I don't want to be your friend, I just want to be your lover . . .

As the song faded, I realized something was strange.

Jamie was completely still.

He'd fallen asleep.

Easing myself out of his embrace, I placed my hand on the face of his heart. I ran my fingers along his cheek, his neck, his chest, peeked beneath his boxers. I bent down and kissed his fresh wound, claiming it as mine. As I caressed his old wounds, some so small and faded that you could only see them up close, with the gaze of a lover, I thought of the artist who'd once kneeled before his naked body like I was and drawn a map of his scars. Surely they had hooked up after, on the floor of an art studio, surrounded by canvas and brushes and mounds of sculpting clay waiting to be born. Jamie may have posed for her, but he had bled for me. He had brought me to a Theater of Dreams.

I decided to wake up sleeping beauty with a passionate kiss.

But first, a little more Malbec. As I reached for the wine, I noticed Jamie's phone next to it and checked the time: 10:33 p.m. I had to get out of here, preempt any maternal worries by texting my mother that I was on my way back.

"Jamie," I said, shaking him awake. "We gotta move."

III.

The Dawn of Separation

Twenty-Two

OMG IT WAS AMAZING!!!!!!!!!!!!!!!!!!!! I texted Farah.

good

Ill tell all about it when I cu. We didn't

do it, but came pretty close. Best night of my life!

cool

Normally I would have been hurt at her lack of enthusiasm, but I was still high from last night. I hummed "House of Cards" on my walk to work. I took the long way through the park and skipped across the stone bridge. I sat on Mrs. Joan Milton's bench and waited for my rose.

But he was late. Really late. So late that by the time I caught sight of him, dashing up the hill from the parking lot, I wasn't so high anymore.

"Sorry," he said. "I had to drop Aunt Marianne at the doctor's and we missed it and the next U-turn was like two miles."

Why did Aunt Marianne have to see a doctor this week, of all weeks?

"It's okay," I said, even though it sucked.

"We better unload," he said.

By the time we were done, it was 3:55 and the line was already five deep. Word had spread that this was the shack's last week. Yesterday the pies were gone in half an hour.

"Let's do something after work today," I said.

"I'd love to hang with you, Morning Dew, but I have to drive Aunt Marianne to Philly to see a dying friend."

Damn Aunt Marianne and her dying friends.

"When do you leave? Saturday?" I asked.

"Thursday evening," he replied.

I assumed he was confused. "Friday is the last day of the shack," I reminded him.

"I know. My friends rented a cabin in Tahoe for the weekend, so I'm heading out early. Aunt Marianne will deliver the pies Friday."

"And you're going home from there?"

"Home, then back to school. When do you leave?"

"Not till the end of the summer," I replied, feeling stunned. If he left Thursday, that meant we had only two days left.

Jamie gripped my waist, bringing me closer. "Hey, don't look so sad."

"I can't help it."

He kissed me. We hugged, and I held him as tightly as I could without cutting off his circulation, but nothing could stop Jamie from moving, except sleep.

"I'll see you tomorrow," he said.

But I didn't want tomorrow. I wanted fall break, I wanted emails and chats and long weekends and summers. I wanted phone calls and sexting. I wanted happily ever after.

"Okay," I said.

The pies sold out in a record twenty-five minutes. I texted Farah.

Let's hang out

Can't I'm going to see rebel antigone oh yeaaaah

Your mom is letting you

Yeah with my cousin Tariq as chaperone. He already told me I'm not allowed to mosh bc some guy will try to grab my tits. Sick.

guys grabbing tits or him telling you that

both. u know I don't mosh anyway. Mosh pits smell like b.o.

but do they smell worse than my pits after being in this shack for an hour

haha probably not. U shd come, you'll fit right in

with noise canceling headphones and a bottle of aspirin maybe

hater

☺ have fun. don't do anything I wouldn't do

stay cool, qureshi. cu soon.

Twenty-Three

"YOU KNOW, I HAD this weird dream last night," Jamie told me as I lay in his arms, breathing in his aroma of baking and Irish Spring soap, a sweet, masculine scent that reflected the essence of my beloved.

"What happened?"

"I was on this high-speed train, going through Transylvania, and the train came to a sudden stop, luggage, babies flying everywhere. Then the train was attacked, except the attackers kind of looked like White Walkers, you know, from *Game of Thrones*, and they had ray guns, and every time they hit someone the person's head would explode. I got down on the floor and kept telling myself to stay still like your uncle did, but you know me, of course I can't, and then someone nudges me and I look up and it's your uncle, he kind of looks like a White Walker except he's brown and wearing a turban, and he points his gun at me and says, 'This is what happens when you can't play dead.' And then boom! I woke up and for a second or two I wasn't sure if I was dead or alive."

I had no idea what to make of this dream. "My great-uncle doesn't look like a White Walker. Or a brown version of a White Walker, or whatever."

"No need to get defensive, MD," Jamie said, stroking my hair. "Dreams are supposed to be screwed up. But it made me think, you know, I've done a lot of things, jumped off cliffs, drag raced, stuff that could have killed me, but that was my choice. I've never had death come at me like that, like it did to him."

It wasn't death that came at Chotay Dada, I thought, it was a mob of men, fueled by a long, brutal history of colonization and subjugation. Farah would have given him one of her lectures, but I wasn't her, and anyway it was too complicated to explain, and I didn't know enough about it.

"And then I was awake for a while, thinking," he continued, "and I started wondering, do they still drink the water from the well?"

"What?"

"The pregnant woman, your uncle's lover, she killed herself by jumping into the well, right? Do the people keep drinking water from it, or is it considered cursed or something?"

"I don't know, I guess they kept drinking it," I answered, trying not to sound as annoyed as I was. I didn't want to spend our second-to-last day talking about Chotay Dada, or Partition. I didn't want to talk about the past. I wanted to talk about the future—*our* future.

"So when's the last time you jumped off a cliff?" I said.

"I cliff dived last year," Jamie said. "Do they have some kind of ceremony, to make the well clean again?"

"Like do they wear scary animal masks and dance in a circle around it, chanting?"

"Is that what they do?"

"No. I was kidding."

Jamie grinned, kissed my nose. "Funny. I'm going to miss our talks. I'm going to miss you."

He checked his pocket watch.

"Ten minutes," he announced. "Better make the most of it."

We started making out, but I was too distracted to enjoy it. I knew I ought to stop waiting passively for him to say something, and instead share my feelings, tell him I didn't want time or distance to determine the end of Jamie and Morning Dew. That was the brave path, and the one that would leave me most exposed. I didn't know what I'd do if he didn't want to be with me. I didn't know how my heart could recover from such a blow. The status quo seemed easier, but it was also driving me insane.

I promised myself that if he didn't bring up our future before he left tomorrow, I would.

"Are you all right?" Jamie asked. "You seem a little off today."

"I'm sad you're leaving," I said.

"I'm sad I'm leaving, too."

So do something about it, I thought.

"How many people do you think are waiting outside?" he asked.

"Six."

He jumped up, leaned over the display case, looked through the gap in the shutter. "Eight! I should go. Stay clear of White Walkers, brown or otherwise."

"I'll try." I got up to open the shutter, a big *Welcome-to-Andromeda's-Pie-Shack* smile plastered on my face. How did Dino manage to be so damn pleasant every day?

When the pies were gone, I texted Farah.

Jamie's leaving 2morrow! so depressed.

Farah responded with a meme of a guy eating a hot chili, his face turning crimson as the spice hit him, tears spraying out of his eyes. *No Chili, No Cry*, it said underneath.

It didn't make me feel any better.

When I got home, my father was making chai, one of the few domestic tasks he not only did, but did well. He was still dressed in his sleeping outfit, a *shalwar* and a stained undershirt. The ring of hair around his head hadn't been trimmed in ages, the humidity making his curls spool outward.

Sleep is his, pride is his, the nights are his / On whose shoulder your curls lay tangled.

The day of union with Jamie was ending, and I might have to endure the feverish night of separation, desperately yearning for a beloved who was unreachable, wondering if someone else's curls lay tangled across his shoulder.

Shit. My life was on the precipice of becoming an Urdu ghazal.

How could I ensure Jamie stayed mine?

"Ah, Shabnam," my father said, as though I hadn't already been in the kitchen for five minutes. "I found a ghazal of Ghalib's that might be easier for you to comprehend."

"Oh my God," I said.

"Sorry?"

How many times had Jamie asked me for a ghazal? Maybe a ghazal could save my life from resembling one.

"Dad, listen. This is important," I said. "I need you to explain to me the form of a ghazal, right now. I need to write one, in English, tonight."

My father, being who he was, didn't ask why, or for whom, but happily launched into a lecture as I scribbled down notes on the back of the class schedule from my mother's gym.

BASIC NOTES ON THE GHAZAL

Usually 4 to 9 verses (ideally an odd number)

Each verse is 2 lines. Each 2-line verse is thematically independent, can stand on its own.

Closing verse usually mentions the poet's pen name

Common rhyme syllable (fearless, hopeless, heartless, stinging, running, mourning) followed by the refrain

Rhyme scheme:

aa

ba

ca

da

ea

My father gave me an English example of a ghazal that he invented in a matter of minutes, but it took me all night to write mine. I wanted the ghazal to be a poignant expression of my love, I wanted it to speak what my tongue could not. I wanted it to move Jamie so much that he couldn't bear not to see me again, and again, and again.

GHAZAL FOR JAMIE

The nightingale, she lost her voice, calling for you
She gave up on the garden, searching for you

I thought the garden had nothing but thorns. They said,
Stop, wait, because your flower, he's coming for you

Winter will end, summer will bring you your rose
Wild and red, scarred and perfect, unfolding for you

The Theater of Dreams will host your debut
In every chair a ghost, sighing for you

A chemical reaction, an afternoon monsoon,
Every cell in my body, yearning for you

Let's stay out super late, making music, making pie
Watch me naked in the moonlight, dancing for you

I am the nightingale and you are the rose
Come close to my lips, hear me singing for you.

Twenty-Four

JAMIE WAS LATE, AND I'd barely slept, though I was wide-awake and fidgeting from the three cups of coffee I'd had before leaving for work. I'd attempted to mask my exhaustion with literally every item in my make-up bag, but it had proved too much. I wished I could wash my face, start over. I wished I'd had the guts to have this conversation days ago. I leaned against the display case, rubbing excess blush off my cheeks with a worn tissue, picking at the mascara clumps in my eyelashes, the notebook burning inside my back pocket.

This was not the way I wanted to be at our last meeting, jangly and wired and cake-faced.

The door swung open.

Jamie, holding a single bamboo basket.

"Sorry I'm late. I was almost here when I had to go back for this." He handed me the basket.

"Should we get the rest now?" I said.

"No—I mean, yes, we probably should, but this pie's for you."

"Me?" I said.

"I realized we never ended up eating pie that time you came over, so I baked one for you last night. Blackberries, your favorite."

"It's my father's favorite—but also mine," I added quickly, not wanting to seem unappreciative, touched to think that we'd both spent last night creating things for each other.

"Race you," he said.

I chose to walk, my stomach roiling from nerves and caffeine overload, and he ran in circles around me. When he started to sing "The Sound of Music" in a falsetto voice, I laughed. It felt good to laugh. It made it harder to be scared.

Fifteen minutes later, the pies were in the display case, their names written on the giant notepad, the notepad on the easel. Jamie had his arms around me, his lips in my hair.

Everything in its right place.

We started making out, his hand sliding around to the small of my back, but once again I was too distracted to enjoy it. The notebook in my pocket burned more than his lips; I wouldn't be able to relax until I gave him my gift, until I knew its outcome.

As he kissed my neck, I said, "I brought something for you too."

"You did?"

"You told me you wanted a ghazal," I said as I handed him the Moleskine notebook. "The first few poems are my father's translations of Faiz, and the last one is a ghazal. I wrote it for you."

"You wrote a ghazal for me? Awesome." He flipped to the final poem, and read, 'Ghazal for Jamie.'"

He read it to himself as I watched, terrified. By the time he was done, I'd be stripped of pretense, the lover lying naked and shivering and hopeful at the doorstep of her beloved's heart.

Jamie looked up from the page, stricken. "Wow, MD. I don't even know what to say."

Say you love me. Say you want to be with me. Say you are my rose.

"It's the nicest thing anyone's written for me. I love it."

"Good," I said, pleased, waiting for more.

"I'm really gonna miss you," he said.

He leaned in for a kiss, but I turned my cheek, determined to continue the conversation.

"We could see each other again," I said.

"We will see each other again," he replied.

"When?"

He shrugged, twirling one of my curls. "I don't know. I leave those things up to fate."

"But maybe we could . . . plan something, you know, like I could come visit you in Madison."

"Oh. Okay." He nodded, as if to indicate he understood, then palmed my face, tilting it upward. “Hey, I loved being with you this summer. Listening to you and learning from you and holding you, it was like a rush all the time. But I’m going back to school, and you’re moving to Philly. It’s always better to end things on a high note, don’t you think? The Theater of Dreams, that was *our* night.”

What the hell did that even mean?

It meant he didn’t want to see me again. It meant he’d always thought of us as a summer fling.

The lover reeled back as the beloved slammed the door in her face.

I was so stupid to think a poem could make him love me.

“Hey, hey, don’t be so sad,” he said.

“Are you sure?” I exclaimed. “Are you sure you want this to end?”

“Nothing really ends,” he said softly.

I could kill him. “It will end if we don’t see each other.”

“I’ll always carry the memory of you with me.”

“Wow,” I said, and then I couldn’t speak.

Don’t cry don’t cry don’t

Jamie wiped the corners of my eyes. “Hey, beautiful, you’re killin’ me with these tears.”

“Please please stop talking,” I said, and spent the next five minutes weeping on his bony shoulder. He held me, stroked my hair, whispered hush and it’s going to be all right and don’t cry, my sweet girl, which only made me cry harder.

The whole while, the voices outside increased, became louder. *Is this really the shack's last summer?* I heard someone ask.

"Morning Dew?" he said gently. "It's after four."

Fuck four, I thought. Fuck love, fuck all of it.

We parted, still holding hands. The cut he'd gotten breaking the window was starting to scab over. Soon it would be an old wound, and I'd still be bleeding.

"Thank you so much for the ghazal, the poems," he said.

"Yeah."

"Can I get a kiss before I go?"

He kissed me, the kind of sweet, tender kiss that reeks of goodbye.

Then he left and I sold pies, smiling so hard it hurt, scraping my nails into my palms to keep from crying.

Twilight on the night of union.

The dawn of separation begins. The nightingale loses her rose.

Twenty-Five

I WENT HOME, LOCKED myself in my room, called Farah. She didn't pick up. I couldn't even cry, because when my mother returned from work she might come up and say hello, and if she realized I was upset, she'd never leave me alone. No tears, no best friend. I was in breakup purgatory.

My mother did come to my room but I was able to act normal enough to keep her visit brief. My phone rang at last. "Father and Son" by Cat Stevens, aka Yusuf Islam. I'd never heard of Cat/Yusuf until Farah introduced me. Mushy singer/songwriter tunes were her dirty secret.

"Where have you been?" I demanded.

"Salaams to you, too. Everything cool?"

"No! Today I gave Jamie a ghazal I wrote basically telling

him I loved him, and he said he loved the ghazal, but that he didn't want to see me again. He said if we did see each other again, it would be because *fate* brought us together. He said he'd always carry the memory of me with him. The *memory* of me."

Farah was silent.

"Farah! Just say it."

"Say what?"

"I told you so."

"I didn't want this to happen."

"But you figured it would. You never liked him."

"This is on him, Qureshi, not me."

This was true, but he was gone, and she was the only other person who knew how much I loved him. "Sorry. I don't mean to attack you."

"So don't."

"Farah, I can't fight with you right now. I'm a mess." I started to cry, the phone cradled between pillow and ear, Big Muchli tucked against my chest.

"It's going to be okay."

"No, it's not. I think he's at the airport," I said. "I want so badly to call him, like maybe if I ask him one more time—"

"Don't call him," Farah said sharply.

"Why not?

"Because he's a manipulative jerk who doesn't deserve a phone call, or you."

"Manipulative jerk?" I was the one whose heart he'd stomped

on, and even I wouldn't call him that. She was way too harsh. What guy could live up to her standards?

Farah made this pained sound. "Listen, I can't talk right now."

"What the hell is going on with you?"

"My parents are fighting."

"So? They're always fighting, that's like their baseline."

When Farah didn't reply, I said, "Listen, I'm so screwed up I don't even know what I'm saying. Can you come over, please?"

"I can't today."

"Tomorrow? Please. I need you."

Silence, then, "All right. Tomorrow."

I made her swear by Allah she would definitely come before I let her go, and then I cried some more into my pillow. I'd skipped dinner, which meant at some point my mother would knock on my door holding a plate of food, and there was no way to disguise the fact that I'd been crying. I needed an excuse for my tears, so I did something I'd been meaning to do for a while. I Googled Bosnian genocide.

After reading about mass graves, systemic rape, and concentration camps, I suddenly didn't want to be alone anymore, but if I went to my mother, she'd ask me too many questions, smother me with overbearing concern.

So I sought out my father instead.

"Entry," he said when I knocked on the study door.

I was such a wreck that even he noticed. "Is something wrong?"

"Have you heard of Srebrenica?" I asked.

My father blinked. "Are you referring to the largest massacre in Europe since the Holocaust?"

I nodded, sinking into the armchair, pulling two pens and a potato chip bag out from underneath my butt. "It's horrible. It's all so horrible."

"Did you expect it wouldn't be?" my father said.

"No, I don't know . . ." I didn't know why I'd come to my father seeking comfort. I didn't know what I was doing, saying. All I knew was that the world was a terrible place that murdered innocent children and offered no salve to the brokenhearted except time.

I was better off alone.

"I came to tell you there's blackberry pie in the fridge," I informed him. "Try not to eat it all at once. I'm going to bed."

I was in my room less than five minutes before my knob rattled.

"Shabu? Open the door."

Goddammit. The one night I wanted my father not to care, and he'd gone and told my mother.

When I opened the door, my mother hugged me. It felt nice to be inside her arms. I wished we could remain in this comforting, nonverbal embrace, but she pulled away, hands on hips, and said, "Why have you been reading about the Bosnian genocide?"

"Because I found out Dino is a refugee," I said.

"Oh. Well, don't read about such things, especially not at night. It will only make you sad."

"Do you know it went on for three years before NATO intervened?" I said. "The whole world watched all those people die. The world didn't care. It pretended to care, but it didn't really. It never really cared."

"It's all right," my mother said, patting my back. "It's over now."

"No it's not. What about all those people who died? What about all those women who were raped? What about the ones who survived? Suffering doesn't stop just because something ends."

"I know that terrible things happen," my mother conceded. "But there's also a lot of good in the world. You have to focus on that."

"I can't! I'm not like you, Mom. I can't push my pain under the rug and pretend that everything is awesome when it isn't."

"Shabu, is something else going on?" my mother said. "Did you fight with Farah?"

"No."

"Then what is it?"

"I told you, it's Bosnia."

"You know you can talk to me about anything."

Ha. When I died, there ought to be two obituaries, one of Shabnam Qureshi and the other of the Shabnam Qureshi her mother never knew.

My back pocket vibrated. I'd been keeping my phone there, in case Jamie called or texted to say he really did love me, that he'd changed his mind.

I had to see if it was him.

"I'm fine now," I told my mother. "I was reading about all that awful stuff and it upset me, but you're right, I need to focus on the positive. Like, if there was no genocide, then Dino wouldn't have come here, and then there'd be no Ye Olde donuts. See, silver lining! You know, I'm tired, I think I'm gonna go to bed."

"You still seem upset," my mother said.

"Mom, please. I'm fine."

"All right, I'll go if you promise to come to me if you feel sad again."

"I promise."

She was almost to the door, the phone almost out of my pocket when she stopped and said, "Listen, I'll need your help next Saturday. Chotay Dada arrives Saturday night."

"Chotay Dada?"

"Yes."

"He's coming back?" I exclaimed. "Why is he coming back?"

My mother frowned. "Why are you asking in that tone? He's staying one night here because his return flight to Pakistan is from JFK."

"Great," I said. "Perfect."

"What do you have against him? He's a nice man."

Chotay Dada had been here when Jamie and I began, and now he returned at our bitter end. My summer fling, bookended by my prayer-bead-happy great-uncle. As if there weren't enough people in this house who didn't understand me.

I sighed. "I don't have anything against him. I need to be

alone, that's all. I need to process."

"Process what? Talk to me."

She'd never leave, she'd keep asking me question after question, on the false assumption that I could actually confide in her, when all I wanted to do was see if my beloved had texted me or not.

My mother was so frigging clueless it was making me crazy. I felt like I was going to explode.

And I did.

"Can you stop asking me to talk?" I cried. "Why do you want to talk all the time? I don't always want to talk to you. Sometimes I want to listen to music, or sit in silence. Why is that so hard for you to understand?"

Her brown gazelle eyes widened, glistening with tears.

Normally, I would have backed off immediately, but I had had the shittiest day of my life, and it was insane that she even imagined we could be friends. She wore old lady underwear and didn't use tampons and begged Allah's forgiveness after she'd accidentally had rum cake at last year's office Christmas party. She wanted me to confide in her but she never confided in me, about the miscarriages or about how difficult it was to be married to a man like my father. She never dared admit how much it could suck to have an emotionally absent husband and a resentful, rebellious daughter.

Maybe I was a liar, but she was, too.

"Listen," I said. "Even if there was something to talk to you about, I wouldn't do it with you or Dad, because neither of you really get me."

"Of course I get you," my mother said. "You're my baby, my Shabu, my little miracle—"

"Stop calling me that! I am not your miracle!"

"Of course you are," my mother said. Actual tears were sliding down her cheeks, but I didn't care. She always wanted to cut things off before they got ugly, keep every conversation nice.

So I made it ugly. I went there.

"I'm not your miracle, I'm just a regular screwed-up teenage girl, and I can never make up for the fact you wanted a boatload of kids and only got me, and I can never make up for the four kids you lost, and you know what—I hate those Precious Moments dolls! They make me want to puke. And if they're supposed to represent all my dead siblings, I've got news for you—your dead babies were brown, not white, blue-eyed, vapid-looking angels!"

By the end, I was shouting. My mother stood for a moment, blinking, stunned, and then fled, closing the door behind her.

I checked my phone.

A photo of Danny and Ian on the beach, arms around each other, Danny kissing Ian on the cheek. **U were right, Qureshi**, Ian wrote. **Together at last!**

Delete.

Twenty-Six

I STARED GUILTILY AT the top of the bookshelf.

The angels were gone.

I'd ruined them for her.

I was a terrible person who didn't deserve my mother, didn't deserve love. I was extremely sad but I was also starving. When I opened the fridge, there was the pie Jamie had baked for me, right at eye level.

The absence of angels, the presence of pie. Everywhere I turned, something to haunt me. I was even worse off than the ghazals' wretched lover; as far as I could tell, in Urdu poetry, the lover didn't have parents, or siblings, or best friends. In real life, there wasn't just one relationship that could mess you up. There were a hundred thousand.

I took the pie out. My father had already eaten half, wrapping the wrong half in plastic.

Jamie, you fraud, I thought. You goddamn fraud.

I stabbed the pie with a fork, once, twice. I scooped up its dark insides, stuffed them in my mouth.

Holy shit.

Delicious.

I ate more, and more, and still more. I was actually glad when I started feeling ill, because at least it was something besides sorrow and despair. I had to leave for work in an hour and I wondered if I should try to make myself vomit. I was tempted to call in sick, except that meant calling Aunt Marianne, who scared me.

I needed to stop referring to her as Aunt Marianne. She'd never be my aunt.

Aunt Marianne was already there when I arrived, reading a book on Mrs. Joan Milton's bench, in the same leather capris and embroidered white kaftan she'd been wearing when we met. Her hair was down today, falling past her shoulders in thin white wisps. She seemed a little frailer than before, but her eyes hadn't lost any of their cerulean intensity.

When she saw me, she dropped the book into the straw bag next to her and handed me her keys. "Go unload," she said.

Hello to you, too, I thought.

It was the first time I'd ever unloaded without Jamie sprinting ahead gracefully, doubling back to tease me. *Come on, MD, the quicker we unload, the quicker we kiss.*

It had all seemed so wonderful, so exciting, so sweet. What could I have done to make him want me more? If I'd dressed better, or done my eyeliner like Farah, or had a better body, would it have made a difference?

When I returned to Aunt Marianne, she moved the straw bag to the ground, which I assumed was an invitation to sit next to her. For once, I was too sad to be nervous. Silver lining.

"Did you enjoy working at Andromeda's?" she asked.

"I did," I replied stiffly. "Thank you for the opportunity."

She didn't respond. A squirrel scurried onto the path, regarded us twitchily, and dashed underneath the bench, back onto the field.

Our field, Jamie had called it.

"He told me about your uncle almost dying on the train," she said.

"My great-uncle." Awesome. What else had he told her?

"It's a tragic story," she said.

For a second, I became paranoid that she knew I'd made it up. But she sounded sincere enough.

"Yes, it is," I agreed.

"You seem like a cool girl," Aunt Marianne said. "I'm sorry if you thought I was unfriendly when we first met, but I try to stay out of Jamie's relationships, past, present, future, whatever."

"How did you know it would become a relationship?" I asked.

"Because I know him. I saw how he looked at you. He'd

already told me about this girl with the big brown eyes and the big beautiful curls who'd run away from him at the mall. He was so excited when he saw you at the farmers' market."

God, she'd seen it coming all along, Jamie courting me, me falling in love, his unceremonious departure.

"I'm not the first pie wallah—pie girl this has happened with, am I?" I said.

Aunt Marianne shook her head.

Oh, our lovely shack, not only ours anymore. How many other girls had lain in his arms there, exactly as I had done?

"It's not like that," she said, reading my horrified expression. "You're only the second."

I was the prettiest pie-wallah in a hundred thousand miles, the second time around. Who was the first? Ashley? Amber? Jasmine? I was about to ask, but thought better of it. What good would it do me to know?

"Why didn't you warn me?" I asked.

"I do not, as a policy, get in the way of love," she said. "Who am I to police anyone's heart? Jamie knows how I feel about his actions. That's all I can do. And it could be worse—at least when Jamie's with you, he's *with* you. Half the time young people talk to you and they aren't even listening, they're on one device or another or have headphones plugging up their ears."

"It still doesn't make what he did okay," I argued.

"Did he ever tell you he loved you? Did he ever tell you he wanted something more?" she asked.

"He didn't *not* tell me." It was mortifying to be talking about this. I stared at her bag, the same one Jamie had been carrying when our eyes met at the farmers' market. The book she'd been reading was *Rough Guide to Brazil*.

"Look, I'm not defending my nephew. I love him, but he can be very selfish."

"I loved him too," I confessed.

"I know. I read your poem," she said. "It was beautiful."

I groaned, covering my face with my hands, imagining Jamie giving it to her, Aunt Marianne reading it and thinking, oh, this poor, deluded girl. I'd given Jamie the book to my heart and he'd already started passing it around. God, I hoped he didn't show the ghazal to anyone else.

I wished I could take it back.

"Shabnam," Aunt Marianne said.

I stayed hidden.

"Don't be that way. You should never be ashamed of a poem like that. Writing it was an act of bravery."

"An act of bravery that failed," I reminded her.

"Like I said, I love Jamie but you're better off without him. He still has a lot of growing up to do. Next time, go for a guy five years older. Eh, five years, ten years, they're all so damn immature."

"I'm so stupid," I said.

"Love makes everyone stupid." She sighed. "Why do we love the men we love? I'm seventy-seven years old, and fuck if I know."

I'd never even imagined an old person could be so interesting. As painful as it was, I could sit on Mrs. Joan Milton's bench talking to her until sunset. I was never sure how to talk to old people so I'd always tried not to. I guess I was being ageist, or ignorant.

"Have you ever had your heart broken?" I asked.

"Of course," she said. "When I was young, I had blonde hair, blue eyes, nice tits. A lot of men fell for me because they thought I was a blonde bimbo. But I was rebellious from the start. I couldn't stand to be told what to do. I went through a lot of lovers, had my heart broken, broke some myself, before I found a man who loved me for who I was."

"Did you marry him?"

"No. Marriage isn't for me. He was my great love though. Now that was a love greater than the sum of all my broken hearts."

"But how do you find that? How do you know when it's real?" I asked.

She shrugged. "You girls, they feed you all this Disney princess bullshit, make you think it'll be easy. And maybe it is, for Bob and Molly Sue, high school sweethearts, married fifty years, but for most of us, it's a hard, beautiful road, littered with thorns. But I didn't come here to gab. You should get to work. Here, let me give you your last week's pay."

As she bent over to retrieve an envelope from her bag, I noticed her grimace.

"Are you okay?" I said.

"As Jamie likes to say, pain is inevitable, suffering is optional. That's a bunch of bull, isn't it?" She handed me the envelope.

"So I guess I'll see you around town sometime?" I said.

"You won't," she said curtly, then added, in a softer tone, "You'll be fine. You're a smart girl, and you're stronger than you think."

"Thanks," I said.

After she was out of sight, I looked inside the envelope. Three crisp one hundred dollar bills. More than twice what I was owed. A feminist version of blood money.

Twenty-Seven

"IS YOUR MOM OKAY?" Farah asked when she came over that evening. "I've never seen her like that. She almost looks sad."

"She *is* sad," I said. "I was really mean to her."

"What happened?"

"I don't want to talk about it."

"Okay." Farah took a bag of Hershey's Miniatures out of her purse. "I know it's not Ye Olde, but we'll have to make do," she said, and ripped the bag open with her teeth, chocolates raining down on my feet.

"Thanks," I said, perusing the goods. I hadn't been eating meals, but I'd gone to the store and bought chocolate chip cookies, salt and vinegar potato chips, dried mango slices, and chocolate peanut butter ice cream. The food made me feel better, until it didn't.

I'd gained at least a pound in less than two days, not what you wanted to happen when you were about to start college. Between breaking up and the freshman fifteen, I'd be a water buffalo by May.

I tore open a Krackel and watched as Farah unrolled her hijab turban, reworking it vertically. "What do you think? I'm thinking of experimenting with height."

"It looks like you have a unicorn horn on your head. Or a phallus."

"Ugh." Farah tossed her scarf aside, undid her topknot.

As she shook her hair out, I said, "Rapunzel, Rapunzel." Her magenta was growing out. It was the first time I'd seen her hair mostly black. She'd drawn a small flower at the tip of her widow's peak. It looked like a daisy.

Everything reminded me of Jamie.

"Rapunzel, my ass. I've got barbed wire and a moat around this tower." Farah frowned at the chocolates. "I don't want any of these. I should have gotten Kit Kats. Or Jelly Bellies. Did you know Reese's Peanut Butter Cups aren't made with real peanut butter? I mean, what the hell is it then?"

I stretched facedown on the bed, pushing the chocolates out from underneath me. "Bad week, huh?" Farah said.

"It hurts," I said.

"I'm sorry."

"It hurts so much," I continued. "And Jamie's aunt all but admitted I'm one of a string of broken hearts."

"God. He's such a mofo."

I rolled onto my back, resting my feet on Farah's lap. "But I can't stop thinking about him. Every time my phone buzzes, I run to it like, maybe it's him, maybe it's him. Do you think I gave up too easy? Maybe I should text him, to see what he says."

"No way. He doesn't deserve you. Forget about that dick-wad."

"I can't," I moaned.

Farah made a grrrr noise. "I want to kill him. I wish he were still here so I could find him and rip his face off."

"Jesus, what's up with you? I'm the one whose heart he broke and I'm not that angry."

"I'm angry on your behalf."

"I don't need you to be angry, I need your support," I said.

"I can't do this," Farah announced, lifting my legs and getting up from the bed. "It's giving me heart palpitations."

"What is?"

"Lying to you."

"Lying to me about what?"

She took a step back, wringing her hands. I'd never seen Farah wring her hands. "I wasn't sure what I should do, but I can't keep this inside me, and anyway if I didn't tell you it would be like I was protecting him, and he doesn't deserve that, that piece of—"

"Farah!" I cried, and she looked at me, startled by my vehemence. "Stop telling me what a dick he is and tell me . . . whatever it is that's bothering you."

"Okay." She nodded, picked up a Mr. Goodbar, made a face at it, threw it down, rubbed her palms together, bit down on her lower lip, went back to wringing her hands.

Whatever it was, it was tormenting her.

My body began to clench and fold into itself, bracing for the awfulness to come.

What could she possibly have to tell me about Jamie?

Oh my God.

Deep down, I'd known Jamie was as fascinated by her as he was by me. More, even. But I'd ignored it, because even if he thought she was cool, it wasn't like he'd act on it.

"So there's this thing that happened," she began. "And I had nothing—"

"Don't," I said. "Tell the story first. From the beginning, no bullshit."

"No bullshit," she repeated. "Tuesday night, I went to Trenton, remember, for the Rebel Antigone show. I'm at the show, and it's amazing, and I'm in the back, by myself, rocking out—"

"I thought your cousin went with you."

"He stayed in the car, FaceTiming with his girlfriend, this dental student who lives in Minnesota. They met through Facebook. He told me he wants to get engaged but he needs to see her without her hijab on first so he knows what he's getting into."

"Farah."

"Sorry. So I'm alone at the show, and I'm headbanging so hard I'm hoping my scarf doesn't fly off. Anyway, the scarf is staying on, and the band is awesome, the lead singer has so much charisma, and I'm having the time of my life, and there's a tap on my shoulder. I turn around, and it's Jamie."

"What? He told me he had to drive Aunt Marianne to Philly that night to see her dying friend," I said. Such a blatant lie, right to my face.

"Yeah, well, Aunt Marianne wasn't with him, and apparently by Philly he meant Trenton, and by dying friend he meant Rebel Antigone concert. Anyway, he says 'Hey,' and I'm kind of in shock, so I say, 'Hey,' and then he starts headbanging next to me, and I don't know what to do. I keep dancing for a minute, and then the song ends, and I'm like, I have to get the hell out of here, because he's making me uncomfortable, and I knew you didn't know he was there because you would have told me. So when the song ends, I tell him that I have to go, and he says, 'And miss the rest of this stupendous show?' and I tell him my cousin's waiting for me outside, and he says, 'Well, in that case, I don't have much time,' and then he . . ." Farah threw up her hands. "Then he tried to kiss me."

oh God. oh God oh God oh God.

My heart had sank. I'd always thought that was a figure of speech, but I could literally feel my heart descending with each and every word.

"And I said, 'Jamie, no,'" Farah continued. "And then he tried again."

Liar Jamie. My lying Jamie. Lying liar pants on fire Jamie.

"I ran away, left the club, got into my cousin's car, hung up his call, and told him we had to get out of there fast. When he asked me why, I told him the mosh pit started getting ugly and I was worried a fight would break out, which sucks because he totally told his mother who told my mother, but anyway. I haven't seen Jamie or heard from him since. That's it, that's all of it. No bullshit."

Farah kneeled next to the bed, touched my waist gingerly. "Are you okay?"

"What do you think?"

"I'm so sorry, Qureshi. I had no idea . . . the whole thing was so surreal, except it was real. But the guy you love, he doesn't exist. The real Jamie isn't an honest person."

"I can't believe it. How could he? He was so nice to me. He listened, he made me feel special. God. I wrote him a ghazal," I said, knocking the sides of my head with my hands. "So stupid. So stupid."

Farah grabbed my wrists, holding them down so I couldn't hit myself. "You weren't stupid. He was really charming and manipulative. Who stands a chance against that combination?"

"You did."

"And if I decide one day that I do want to get married, who knows what douchebags I'll meet? As far as I know, there's no matrimonial service with a 'no douchebag' guarantee."

"You would never use a matrimonial service."

"Never say never."

"I can't believe he made up a dying friend!"

"Yeah, you guys had a lot of fake death for such a short relationship," Farah noted.

I hadn't told Farah the annoying things he'd done that I'd forgiven him for, like what he said to Dino, or his dream that turned Partition into a fantasy video game, because I wanted to protect him, because I didn't want Farah to think badly of him. Ha. What a goddamn joke.

I loved him, and he hit on my best friend.

Is it real, or merely a a web / Spun by the spider of my delusion

It was never real. It had always been a delusion.

I pulled my phone out of my pocket, unlocked it with angry jabs. "I'm going to tell him off, that lying bastard, that piece of sh—"

"Hey." Farah yanked the phone away. "You can't call him right now, you're too upset. You'll scream incoherently and start to cry. If you want to call him, wait for the rage to subside, then think carefully about what you want to say, so that you can completely eviscerate him."

"Eviscerate him," I repeated. "Yeah."

"I'll give you your phone back, but you have to swear by Allah you won't call him tonight," she warned me. "Or even tomorrow."

"What Allah?" I said.

"Fine. Swear by your mother's life."

"I've already ruined my mother's life."

"Oh for God's sake, just take it back," she said.

"Put it on my desk."

She opened a desk drawer and shoved it beneath all the papers and pens, as if that might further deter me.

"That day, after we all hung out, he asked me what your hair was like," I said. My voice was so hollowed out with pain I could barely recognize it. "I meant to say it was thick but instead I said it was limp, because I didn't want him to think about you more than he already was. God. I'm so stupid."

"Stop saying that! Trusting someone isn't stupid! It's how you should be. He's the one who's screwed up, not you."

"Yeah."

"Hey." She pressed her forehead to mine. "Are you angry with me?"

I wasn't angry with Farah. I trusted her. I knew she'd never betray me like that. Except.

I pulled back. "Why didn't you tell me that night? After it happened?"

"I didn't know what to do," she confessed. "I was still in shock when I got home from the concert. I thought of calling you, but I thought, what if he denies it, and you don't believe me?"

"I'd always believe you," I said.

"I know, but it would be like, your beloved versus your best friend. I knew he was leaving in two days, so I decided to wait and see what happened. I figured if you guys stayed together, I'd tell you. And if you didn't stay together, I figured I'd play it by ear, because I didn't want to hurt you, or for you to be mad at me, and things have already been so fucked up between us. But you know me, I'm a shitty liar. And then when you were talking about texting him . . . I'm so sorry. It sucks. He sucks." Farah pretend-spat over her shoulder.

"Have things been that fucked up between us?" I said. "I mean, I know we haven't talked about what happened, but I didn't think we were that bad."

"We . . ." Farah shook her head. "Let's not talk about us now. You've got enough going on."

"You might as well pile it on," I said.

"I don't want to pile it on," she protested. "I want you to feel better."

"I want to know the other stuff you haven't said," I insisted. "About us. No more secrets. I'm done with pretending. I'm done with secrets."

"Do you seriously want to talk about this now?" Farah asked, incredulous.

"I'll start. You hate me because you feel like I abandoned you," I declared.

"I don't hate you."

"But you're pissed."

"I'm hurt," she said. "But—"

"Stop it," I exclaimed. "Stop tiptoeing around it because you feel sorry for me. Bring it. I'm serious. Honesty hour starts now."

"Well, I think it started like twenty minutes ago."

"Farah!"

"Fine. I . . ." Farah walked over to the window, rapped her knuckles against the glass. "I don't think I'm ready to have this conversation."

"I'll start then," I said. "I made out with Ryan. Even though I knew he was a douche. Even though I knew it would hurt you, maybe even because I knew it would hurt you. I was in a Jacuzzi, and I was already tipsy, and we drank champagne, and he was half naked, and I kissed him. And then I lied to you about it."

Farah didn't turn around. "It's okay."

"No, it's not," I said. "You suspected. You were pissed."

"I was pissed way before Ryan."

"Why?"

"You sure you want to do this?"

"Yes."

Farah surveyed the room, walked over to the chair, tipping it so the clothes fell off, sat down across from me, took a deep breath. "You know, if you chose to wear a paper bag over your head, I would have your back. But when I needed you most, you bailed. You didn't even want to stand close to me. And even when you did, you weren't really there. I could feel it from the beginning, how tense you were, how you only relaxed when you and I were alone in your house. I was really hurt, but the day you laughed at Ryan's dumbass joke, that day you broke my heart. I mean, I know we're not nightingale and rose, but friendship is a kind of love, isn't it? I felt like you betrayed me."

She was right. I did betray her. I was a terrible, terrible person.

"Remember when you came to see me, at the *masjid*?" she continued. "We'd barely spoken in a while, and you came up to me as if nothing had ever happened, forget about sorry, you didn't even ask me how I was doing."

I tried to recall our conversation. "I didn't?"

"No. At first, I thought you'd come to apologize, but instead you launched right into what you needed from me, which was listening to how in love you were. Since we started talking again, it's been all about you."

"Why didn't you say something? Why didn't you tell me how upset you were?" I said.

"I don't know. You've been so busy with Jamie I've hardly seen you anyway. And when we did meet, you were taking up all the space, and it never felt like the right time to rock the boat. But, listen, even though, yeah, I was mad at you, I never in a million years wanted to hurt you. If I'd known what Jamie was going to do, I would have skipped the show."

"I know," I said. "Did he mention me at all that night?"

"No. We hardly talked before he . . . went for it."

One night, we were hooking up in the Theater of Dreams. The next night, he was trying to kiss Farah. And the next day, I'd lain in his arms, listening to his stupid dream.

"Are you okay?" Farah asked.

"I think I'm going to be sick."

She jumped up, brought over my wastebasket. I shook my head. "I'm not really going to. But I think I need to be by myself right now."

"You sure?"

"Yeah."

"Okay. I love you. Call me whenever, wherever."

I was alone again. I uncurled my toes, unclenched my fists, shook out my arms, forcing myself out of the rigor mortis of despair. Then I wept.

And wept.

I wept until I had nothing left, until every last memory of Jamie and me reeked of salt.

Twenty-Eight

THE GREAT URDU POET Mirza Ghalib once wrote, "Though sorrow is life-destroying, we cannot escape it, as we have a heart."

Goddamn heart.

I didn't leave my room all day on Saturday. In the evening, my mother set a plate of hot food outside my door, knocked, and disappeared, a gesture which made my sorrowful heart splinter with remorse. I wasn't sure if I'd ever be okay again, but I knew nothing would be okay if I didn't make up with my mother, a woman so kind that even when you were mad at her you still wanted to hug her.

Sunday 10:00 a.m. My mother was right where I thought she'd be, on the couch, watching *Cooking and Conversation with*

Yasmeen Bhatt. Every week Yasmeen made one dish with a Pakistani celebrity. She had definitely had a face-lift: her skin, always heavily layered with makeup, stretched good and tight across her bones. Depending on who the celebrity guest was, she did more flirting than cooking, but my mother said her recipes were always good.

It had been three days since we'd spoken, which was completely insane.

"Hi," I said.

"Hi." My mother had a green face mask on, which cracked as she smiled.

I knew that if I didn't mention what happened, she wouldn't either, that she'd already forgiven me, that I didn't need to apologize. Except she deserved an apology, and I wouldn't let her settle for less.

"Can I join you?" I asked.

"Of course," she replied, patting the cushion next to her.

I practically ran to the couch, curling up next to her, my head against her chest. Oh, to be five again, when your mother's embrace truly could make everything all right.

"I missed you," my mother said, squeezing my shoulder.

"Listen, Mom," I said. "I'm sorry I said those things. I'm sorry I was rude about your angels. You should put them back."

"It's all right. They do look a bit silly," my mother replied.

"Okay, they kind of do, but I shouldn't have said it. And I shouldn't have yelled at you."

"It's okay."

"No, it's not okay. You can say it, you know, that what I did was horrible. That I broke your heart. That the family you have isn't the family you wished for. It's okay to be sad. I know your life is good compared to the women you help, but you're allowed to feel sorry for yourself sometimes."

"I know that."

"Then how come you never act sad? How come you're always so nice, and grateful? Dad can be a crappy husband, and I can be a crappy daughter. I mean, does that never bother you? Be honest."

My mother muted Yasmeen Auntie and her handsome actor guest. "Oh, Shabu. Yes, it's true I always imagined a big family. Sometimes, when I'm in the grocery store and I see a mother shopping with her three children, I do feel a little sad. But this is my life. You and Dad are who I love. I wouldn't trade you two. And hey, at least one of you knows my birthday."

It took me a moment to realize she was kidding. "Wow, Mom, that was pretty funny."

"Thank you," she said.

"Dad has no idea how lucky he is," I declared.

"Maybe not," she conceded. "And you? Are you all right? You still haven't told me why you were so upset."

Even in this genuinely tender mother-daughter moment, there remained a gaping chasm between us. Would there ever be a day when I felt comfortable talking to my mother about matters of love, and heartbreak, and betrayal?

"I was fighting with Farah," I told her. "I wasn't very supportive of her when she started wearing hijab, and we fell out, and then we became friends again, but there was still tension because I never said I was sorry, and she never said how upset she was with me, but it's okay, we're going to work it out."

"Good," she said. "Farah and you are too close not to stay friends. *Are*—the *saag gosht* is already done."

She unmuted Yasmeen Bhatt, who was ladling a spinach and goat dish onto plates. "Look what you made!" she exclaimed, nudging the handsome actor.

"Don't tell my wife," he warned her. "She'll stick me in the kitchen."

Twenty-Nine

FARAH KEPT TEXTING TO check in, and I texted her back, but, even though I needed to apologize to her, too, I wasn't quite ready. I'd thought my life was one thing, and then I found out it wasn't that at all, and having to recast everything in the light of what I now knew was a form of torture. I looked at photos of Jamie, selfies of us, remembered his compliments, his kisses, his gaze, his touch. How could he do and say all that he did, with such intensity and sincerity, and turn out to be such a liar? I assumed people capable of such betrayal wouldn't seem so nice, like you'd talk to them and you'd be able to sense their dishonesty. But Jamie had me completely fooled. And it wasn't like he'd hit on some random girl. He'd gone after my best friend. Who knows, maybe he'd hit on random girls, too, and I just didn't know.

I'd love to hang with you, Morning Dew, but I have to drive Aunt Marianne to Philly to see a dying friend.

I'd been so naive.

How could I trust anyone again? If only you could see into people's hearts, know if they were true.

I came close to calling Jamie at least ten times a day, but changed my mind at the last second. I wanted to eviscerate him, but I was in too much pain to think straight. When it was time, I knew Farah would help me with the words.

A week later, when I texted her asking if she could meet me at Ye Olde later, she responded immediately.

Hell yeeeeeeeeeeeeeessss!

It was my first time in Ye Olde since I'd come with Jamie, and the first time I'd come with Farah in ages.

As soon we stepped inside Dino called out, "Shabnam! Farah! Hello!" the rest of the line turning to look at us.

We waved back, minor celebrities in the world's greatest donut shop. It felt good to be together again in our old haunt, like we were reclaiming a part of our history, one that hadn't been tainted by the guy I'd loved.

When we got to the register, Dino said, "I'm so happy to see you ladies here together. Today's donuts are on me."

"No way," Farah said as we both took out cash.

"I won't accept it," Dino said.

"But your tip jar will," she shot back, stuffing a ten inside.

"All right, you win," Dino said, then pointed to her head. "Nice style."

He was referring to how she'd managed to wrap her headscarf into two buns on either side of her head.

"Thanks. It only took me forty-five minutes to get it right," Farah said.

"Well, it looks very good." Though we assumed Dino, being Bosnian, was probably Muslim, he never brought it up and neither did we. When Farah started wearing her headscarf, he hadn't praised her or questioned her or raised his eyebrows. All he'd said was, "New look."

"You should do a YouTube tutorial on how to tie your scarf like Princess Leia's hair," I suggested.

"There already is one," Farah said.

"Is that so?" Dino replied.

"You have no idea," Farah told us.

The guy behind us coughed politely, and we quickly ordered two donuts and two American coffees. Dino asked me, "How is your friend Jamie?"

"He's not my friend anymore," I said.

"Oh. Sorry to hear this," Dino replied.

"She's better off without him," Farah declared, and Dino gave me this kind, crooked smile that made me want to cry and reach across the register and hug him.

As I went to the jukebox to line up Radiohead, waving at the old Bosnian men playing cards, I had this crazy thought, about how Dino must have witnessed terrible atrocities but still exuded such happiness, how Dino was the kind of guy my mother should have married, because they shared the same depth of kindness, and cared about other people, and they would have cared for each other in the same way, and grown old happily.

Except then of course I wouldn't exist.

"What are you thinking about?" Farah asked when I returned to our table.

"About how my mother would have been happier if she'd married Dino."

"Your father's not so bad."

"He's great to talk to about Urdu poetry, not so great to be married to."

"He's better than my dad. Plus, your mom's a saint, so very few men would be worthy of her."

"Exactly," I said. "Hence Dino."

"Ah. I see your point. But how do we know Dino doesn't have a dark side? Like maybe he has a secret gambling habit. Or is really into monster truck races. Or BDSM."

"Dino?"

"Yeah," Farah conceded. "He's probably always nice. He doesn't wear a wedding ring; maybe he and your mom still have a chance."

"My mom would never leave my dad. He wouldn't survive one week on his own. And it's not like I want her to. My dad's an idiot, but I love him, too. I just wish . . ."

"What?" Farah prodded.

I sighed. "Before this summer, I didn't pay much attention to my parents' marriage. Maybe ignorance is bliss. Maybe it's better not to know."

Farah folded her hands, one of which was decorated with an intricate peacock, drawn in electric blue. "Do you think it would be better for you not to know about Jamie?"

"No," I said. "It destroyed me, but I'm glad I know the truth."

"Listen, I want to say again—"

"Wait," I interjected. "Before we talk about him, I want to start with us."

"Okay. Let's start with us, and the peanut butter Nutella," Farah said, breaking apart the donut.

I didn't touch my half; I couldn't indulge until I'd apologized properly.

"So I've been thinking about why I bailed on you," I began, "and there's the obvious reason, that I was embarrassed by all the attention. For you it's this big political statement, and it's your identity, but being Muslim doesn't feel like a big part of who I am. I mean, I don't think about it as I'm going about my everyday life like you do. It doesn't move me like it moves you. I wasn't ready for all the attention, for people to assume I was religious too because I was your BFF. But I was thinking about it more, and I realized there's another reason, too. I was hurt when you started wearing hijab, because I felt a little betrayed."

"Betrayed?" Farah said, the gravity of the word prompting

her to set down her donut. "By what?"

"You said yourself it was such an important decision. But I'm your best friend, and you didn't talk about it with me at all. I found out when you walked into school, along with everyone else. I was hurt that you didn't include me, or even give me a heads-up. But instead of talking to you about how I felt, I let it simmer inside me, which wasn't fair."

"Right," Farah said. "I can see why that would piss you off. I guess I didn't tell you because I was worried you wouldn't support it, that you would try to get me to change my mind."

"Since when do I have so much sway over what you do?" I joked.

She smiled. "I'm not saying I would have changed my mind. Do you think, if I had talked to you about it beforehand, you would have behaved differently?"

"I don't know," I replied honestly. "I'd like to say yes, but maybe I would have done the exact same shitty thing. Anyway, the point is, I'm sorry I wasn't there for you like I should have been, and I never want to hurt you like that again. I'm sorry I kept questioning your choice instead of supporting it. And I'm also sorry I busted back into your life and talked about myself constantly like a selfish idiot. God, I was worried about Jamie not seeing me, and didn't realize all the things I wasn't seeing about myself. Anyway, if I ever do that again, will you call me out on it? I mean, I hope I won't, but if I do . . ."

"Yeah," she said. "I will."

"And I think we should promise each other that if we're ever angry again, we'll talk to each other about it right away."

"Definitely," she agreed. "What should we swear on?"

"Something secular."

"How about pinkies?"

As we linked fingers, I said, "I'm really really sorry."

"No worries, friend. You had me as soon as you texted Ye Olde," Farah joked. "And now I want to apologize."

"For what?"

"When Jamie tried to kiss me, I should have kicked him in the balls, I should have told him off, and I should have told you right away. But I was completely flummoxed. I didn't know what to do. What if he said he loved you and wanted to be with you? And then denied he'd ever kissed me? It would have killed me if you didn't believe me, if you stayed with a guy like that."

"I would have believed you," I swore. "At least, I'm pretty sure I would have."

"This sounds terrible, but I'm really glad he dumped your ass."

I laughed out loud, for the first time in days.

"You totally dodged a bullet," she continued.

"I still don't understand," I said. "What was he thinking, messing with my best friend?"

Even though I'd been laughing a second ago, I could feel the tears coming on. I covered my face with my hands, willing myself not to lose it in Ye Olde Donut Shoppe, where people came to be happy.

"Hey, hey," Farah said, rubbing my arm. "He's a loser who

was thinking only about himself. I think you and I were like the exotic flavors of the month for him."

I wiped my eyes, looked up at the lovely scrolling shadows the glass lamp above our table cast upon the ceiling. "How could I not see it?"

"Because he was charming. And the whole sneaking into the theater thing, I mean, he obviously cared about impressing you. It was a thoughtful, pretty cool thing to do."

"Except he tried to kiss you the next night! All those times he told me how much he loved my curls, how beautiful I was, and I actually believed him."

"I don't think he was lying about that," Farah said.

"Are you serious?"

"We don't live in some 1950s comic book. No one's all good or all evil. He wasn't honest, but it doesn't mean he lied all the time. It doesn't mean he didn't like you, in his own screwed-up way."

"But he liked both of us!"

"At least the man had good taste," Farah said.

We burst out laughing, and Farah slid my donut half toward me. "Eat already."

"I have to go soon," I told her. "I promised my mother I'd help her cook for tomorrow. Chotay Dada is coming tonight, can you believe it? He was there when it all began, and now he's back."

"The infamous Partition survivor returns? Are you going to ask him what really happened?"

"No—why would I?"

"You've lied so much about him, aren't you curious to know the truth?" she challenged.

"Uh, what am I going to say—please pass the biryani and by the way, do you happen to be the sole survivor of a bloody train massacre?"

Farah laughed. "How about, would you like some more water and by the way, did your pregnant lover happen to drown herself in a well?"

Did they still drink the water?

God. I made up lies about Chotay Dada to pique Jamie's interest, and where had it gotten me?

"Can you ask him, please?" Farah said. "What if his story is almost the same as yours? That would be so awful and weird."

"But I hardly know him."

"Well, fictionally you do."

Dino appeared at our table with another donut. "New experiment," he said. "Maple pecan. Give your honest opinion. I think they're a little too sweet."

I hoped he hadn't noticed me almost crying. "Oh, Dino, I've got to lose at least five pounds before college," I demurred.

"Well, I don't," Farah said, and took a bite. "Mmmmmmm."

"Well?" Dino asked.

"Tone the sweetness down a tiny bit, and it will be perfect," Farah told him.

Dino nodded. "As I thought."

"Dino, by the way," I said, "I'm sorry about what happened before, when I came here with Jamie."

"No need for an apology," Dino replied graciously.

"Still, I hope it didn't make you uncomfortable."

"You know," Dino answered, "I was talking to an Iraq war veteran, and he said people always ask him, 'What was the war like?' But how can you answer a question like that? How can you explain something so complex? All you can do is give them a, a sound—"

"Sound bite?" Farah offered.

"Yes, a sound bite," Dino said. "So, when people sometimes ask me, I give them a sound bite. But I was glad that Jamie had heard of the genocide. Many people in your generation don't even know what happened in Bosnia."

A group of leather-clad bikers entered the shop, and Dino excused himself to take their order.

"What did Jamie do to Dino?" Farah asked.

I lowered my voice. "He asked Dino if he was a refugee of the Bosnian genocide. And when Dino said yes, Jamie was like, Cool, can you tell us about it?"

"What? He said *cool*?"

"Uh-huh." I told her the rest of what happened, Farah shaking her head the whole time.

"Of course Dino was totally nice about it. He's still nice about it."

"Bless his heart," Farah said. "Man, Jamie. Such a lame ass.

You should call him up and tell him he inspired Dino to change the name of his shop to Genocide Donuts."

"That's terrible."

But Farah wasn't finished yet. "It could be pastries from places of genocide. Don't feel too bad, citizens of America—the people may have died, but their desserts live on."

"That's really terrible," I said, smiling. "But how come you think what Jamie did was lame but you want me to ask Chotay Dada about Partition?"

"That's different," she explained. "You have a vested interest."

"Which is?"

"Your history. And if he doesn't want to talk about it, he'll say no, right?"

"But what if the mere mention of it gives him PTSD?"

"Dino seems fine."

"Dino's obviously not a typical genocide survivor."

"What is a typical genocide survivor? But seriously, I don't know enough about it. You should do what feels right. I gotta go, too. My mother wants me to scrub the tile grout in the bathrooms tonight."

"What?"

"What can I say? I'm friggin' Cinderella. The first thing I'm going to do when I start making money is hire a cleaning lady. And I will never use white tile grout in my bathroom. Live and learn, Qureshi, live and learn."

As we got up to leave, I noticed that one of the old Bosnian men was singing along to Radiohead's "Karma Police" while staring intently at his card hand. Meanwhile, the four bikers were now sitting in a row at the counter, *Riders on the Storm* written in white cursive across their black jackets.

I was really going to miss this place. In less than a month, I'd be in an unfamiliar place, with unfamiliar people and a wounded, wounding heart, and no Ye Olde donuts.

"You should go on ahead, though," Farah said. "I'm going to quickly check out what's new on the bookshelf."

"Okay—but we didn't even talk about what's going on with you," I said.

"It's okay," she assured me. "You can find updates on my new blog, *Life of a Hijabi Renegade*."

"I'm serious."

"It's cool. We still have the rest of the summer to talk about me."

As we hugged I said, "I love you."

"Love you too, Q."

As awful as it was, at least the Jamie incident had actually brought Farah and me closer together. My black cloud had a true silver lining, and maybe even a promise of sun.

Thirty

I WENT DOWNSTAIRS THE next morning to a scene of déjà vu: my father and Chotay Dada in the dining room, my father grunting disapprovingly behind the *New York Times*, Chotay Dada seated across from him, wearing the same impeccably stiff *shalwar kameez* and leather sandals. Either he had shrunk or my memory had built him up, because I realized he actually wasn't much bigger than me; the fullest thing about him was his beard. The prayer dent in his forehead seemed darker and deeper, like he'd spent most of his time in America in prostration. The orange *tasbih* in his hand, though, was exactly as I remembered.

I set down a plate of glistening puri bread and my mother's homemade tamarind chutney in a silver gravy bowl carved with grapevines.

"*As'salaam alaikum*," I said.

"*Wa'alaikum salaam*," he said. "*Kaisi ho?*"

"Fine," I replied in Urdu.

My mother entered with a bowl of chole, and became immediately distressed that no one was eating. "Take food, please," she insisted, spooning some onto Chotay Dada's plate.

"Why have you cooked so much? You should sit and eat now," Chotay Dada told her.

"I'll come soon," she promised.

"Your mother works too hard," Chotay Dada said.

This prompted me to go into the kitchen to ask if she needed help, but she insisted she was fine and asked me to please talk to Chotay Dada.

When I returned, Chotay Dada's *tasbih* was moving through his fingers, his lips silently forming the same words over and over.

La ilaha illallah.

Karma police arrest this man he talks in maths.

If I hadn't gone to the mall with Chotay Dada, if I hadn't met Jamie, what kind of summer would I have had? I felt like a different person than when he'd first visited. Broken, but determined to put myself back together, hopefully into something stronger.

Chotay Dada completed his *tasbih* circuit, carefully setting the beads next to his plate.

Was what happened to him during Partition very traumatic? He didn't seem traumatized. But then Dino fled a genocide and you'd never guess it. The Holocaust survivors had their number tattoos and museums and lots of Hollywood movies. Actually, the Bosnians had that movie by Angelina Jolie. I'd suggested to my mother we see it once on our movie night, but she refused, saying it would be too depressing, so we'd gone to see *Beauty and the Beast* in 3D instead.

If Angelina were here, she'd ask Chotay Dada what happened to him during Partition. Then maybe she'd make a movie about it.

Come to think of it, Rwanda also had a Hollywood movie.

I realized Chotay Dada was looking at me, and smiled.

"You start college in the fall?" Chotay Dada asked.

"Yes."

"What will you study?"

"History," I replied, an answer that seemingly came from nowhere.

"Very good."

"Thanks."

"With what focus?" he asked, in English.

"South Asian history," I answered.

"Very good," he repeated. "What era? Mughals?"

"I'd like to learn about colonial India, and Partition."

I'd said it. The *P* word had left the building.

"Partition?" Chotay Dada said. "Interesting. Why this?"

Shit. I hadn't expected him to interrogate me. "Well, because it's a monumental event in history, but no one really talks about it."

"This is true." He picked up his fork and stabbed a single chickpea. "Usually, with such things, there is a good guy and a bad guy," he continued. "But Partition, there was no good guy—or bad guy."

"What about the British?" I asked. "Aren't they the bad guys?"

The newspaper lowered, revealing my father's face, his mouth full of food as he said, "Of course they are. Bloody Churchill and the Bengal famine. Three million people starved because of him, and people here call him a hero!"

"Yes, the British were bad," Chotay Dada agreed, "but we still killed each other. The Muslims, the Hindus, the Sikhs, they all did terrible things, had terrible things done to them. I think after it was over, people wanted to forget."

"But how do you forget something like that?" I said.

Chotay Dada was quiet, staring at the framed Picasso print on the wall, two hands holding a bouquet of flowers, and I thought, oh no, I've gone too far.

"I am glad you are studying it," Chotay Dada said. "More people should study it. What is that saying—you must know history to make sure it does not repeat itself."

"Shabnam's studying Partition?" my father said.

"I might, in college."

"Very good," my father stated. "But you can start learning now—Chotay Dada was a boy in Lahore during Partition."

Lahore, not Delhi. My grandfather had lived in Delhi before

Partition, and I'd assumed the same about Chotay Dada. So the setting of my story was wrong. I don't know why this surprised me, when I'd basically been talking out of my ass.

"Why don't you tell her about it?" my father continued.

Leave it to my father to ask the socially inappropriate question, a cringe-inducing trait that actually came in handy once in a while.

"What do you want to know?" Chotay Dada asked me.

This was actually happening.

"Anything," I ventured.

"Tell her how bloody it was," my father insisted.

I was worried this would offend Chotay Dada, but he stroked his beard thoughtfully, his prayer beads dangling from his hand. "The bloodiest thing for me was what happened to our neighbors. I'm sure you know that Lahore was a diverse city for centuries: Sikhs, Muslims, Hindus, Parsis, some Christians, too."

I knew little about Lahore, but I nodded as if I did.

"Most neighborhoods were segregated, but ours was mixed. In the months leading up to August 1947, there were mobs, killings, fires. People were scared, people were dying. It was a very violent time, but there were also times of boredom, when we were shut up in our house playing chess or carrom, waiting for the curfew to lift. Every day more and more Muslim refugees from the Indian side arrived in Lahore. The expressions on their faces . . . there was no more light on anyone's face, not in those who ran, or those who chased, or those who hid. Non-Muslim houses were being marked so when the angry mobs came through they would know which ones to attack. The police were mostly Muslim and did nothing. They even helped sometimes. Our neighbors were Hindus, old friends. Our fathers had grown up together. They played cards together. They always used to bet. We knew when my father won because he'd come home with sweets for us.

"My father was an easygoing man. He was a civil servant but he didn't like politics. He liked to fly kites and play cards. Nor was he a religious man. I learned about religion from my mother. My father didn't agree with what was happening, but he wasn't the type to get involved. You might call him, in English you say *meek*.

"Soon, the non-Muslim families with means were all gone. But my neighbor's wife was on bed rest, about to give birth to her fourth child. The doctor had said she might not survive the journey, so they stayed. One day, the mob arrived. We could hear them chanting. *Maro*, *maro*, kill, kill. My father was at the gate, listening, my mother yelling for him to move away. The chants came closer and stopped in front of our neighbor's house. What my father had been fearing was now right in front of him.

"'Take the children and hide,' my father told my mother."

"'Now, of all times, you decide to be brave!' she said. I'd never seen her so angry, but still my father opened the gate and went next door.

"I remember my sisters and me crying for him to come back, my mother clapping her hands over our mouths."

My mother had arrived in the middle of this story, too compelled by its narrative to interrupt. She was covering her face with a napkin, like she might throw up into it, and my flesh was covered in goose bumps. I didn't know how Chotay Dada could talk about it so calmly.

"We locked ourselves in a room and hid. I was certain the mob would kill my father, we all were. But, a while later, my father came limping home, badly beaten, but alive."

"And your neighbors?" I asked.

"Dead. Parents, children, servants, all dead."

"Bloody Brits," my father spat, and when it became clear that was the end of the story, resumed reading his newspaper.

My mother picked up the serving spoon.

"Some chole?" she said as cheerfully as she could, as if the spoon wasn't trembling in her hands, as if Chotay Dada's plate wasn't already full of chole he'd barely touched.

"I prefer to eat after my morning walk," he said. "I think I'll take it now. Do I have time?"

My mother glanced at the clock. "Yes, the car service isn't coming until noon."

"Good. I won't be long."

I imagined him circling our block alone like he did last time, and it depressed me. Plus I was also a little worried he might keel over in tears. The least I could do was offer him some company and a nice destination.

"Do you like roses?" I said. "There's a really nice rose garden in the park. I could take you there."

"Yes," he said. "That sounds nice."

"But the walk back is uphill," my mother warned.

"That's all right," he assured her. "It will be good for my health."

Chotay Dada went to the bathroom and my mother summoned me to the kitchen. I hopped on a stool and watched as my mother paced around the island, wiping it frantically with a sponge. "Do you think he's all right?" she whispered.

"I don't know, I think so," I said.

"How did this even come up?"

I was about to say my father was the one who asked, but that wasn't exactly fair, because I was the one who'd brought up the topic.

"He's not freaking out," I told her, "so you shouldn't either. You know you're using the dishwashing sponge?"

My mother looked down at the island, now covered with foamy bubbles. She dropped the sponge. "I hope he's okay. Promise you'll only talk about pleasant things on your walk!"

"Happy thoughts all the way."

My mother came over and hugged me, sighing into my hair, squeezing me so hard it hurt.

When Chotay Dada came in, she let go and exclaimed, a little too loudly, "Shabu, Chotay Dada is ready! It's such a beautiful day, what a lovely walk it will be!"

It *was* a beautiful day, and Chotay Dada seemed content to observe the scenery in silence. Sometimes he'd pause to admire a tree, or a well-tended flower bed, or marvel at the gaggle of gnomes in a yard halfway down the hill. It was unusual to see a man like Chotay Dada in our neighborhood, and whenever someone passed us, I made sure to smile and say hello, so they wouldn't perceive us as a threat.

It wasn't until we reached the stone bridge in the park that I realized I was taking a long route to the rose garden, one that would take us by the pie shack. For some reason, I wanted to see it again.

But I wasn't prepared for the stab of pain when I saw it, Mrs. Joan Milton's bench, the dandelion grass we danced upon, Andromeda's plaintive face on the side of the shuttered shack, behind whom Jamie and I had so often kissed. I thought it would all seem darker, uglier, given what I knew, but everything looked the same.

It was me who was different.

"You know this place," Chotay Dada said, his voice startling me.

"Yes," I said. "I worked here this summer, selling pies. I was a pie wallah."

"Good pies?" he asked.

"The best."

We stood looking at the shack in silence a little longer, then he said, "My father's friend, our neighbor, had a daughter, one year younger to me."

"They killed her."

"Yes."

He didn't say that he'd loved her, but he didn't have to.

So he had lost a beloved. Not to a well, but to a mob.

Chotay Dada recited something in Arabic, probably wishing peace on her soul.

I bowed my head, subdued by a sense of perspective. What was my loss compared to his?

"You study history and learn about Partition," he told me. "Write about it so others can learn, too. All the people we lost, they should be remembered."

"I will," I said. It was a weighty promise, and I didn't know if I'd keep it, but I couldn't refuse.

"Good," Chotay Dada said. "And where is this rose garden?"

"Come," I said. "I'll take you there."

Thirty-One

ONE WEEK WENT BY, then another. Some days my heart ached more, others less. Some days I thought of Chotay Dada's story and felt better about my own, other days I still felt sad, or angry, or confused, or everything at once. But I started getting ready to leave for college, which helped, and I saw Farah lots, and I went to the movies with my mother, and hung out with my father in his study, talking about poetry but also trying to make him a better husband.

I made him play social skills games I'd found on the internet with me, coached him on things like asking my mother how her day was, and gave him a book called *How to Improve Your Emotional Intelligence: A Practical Guide.*

"We can read it together," I said.

My father glanced at the table of contents. "How to enjoy talking to anyone," he read. "Nonsense. How can you enjoy talking to people who are stupid?"

"No one's making you talk to stupid people. Do you think I'm stupid? Mom?" I asked, hoping he wouldn't say yes.

"No."

"So will you read this book with me then?"

"Do I have a choice?" he replied.

"Nope."

Toward summer's end, I felt pretty good, excited about the future, coming to terms with the past. I still hadn't contacted Jamie, and he hadn't gotten in touch with me, and though I fantasized about "fatefully" running into him one day, looking slender and lovely, and telling him he was a liar/horrendous person before riding off into the sunset with my awesome new boyfriend, I was beginning to think I wouldn't contact him at all.

"Are you serious?" Farah exclaimed when I told her. "What kind of hot-blooded seventeen-year-old are you? Don't you want to give it to him?"

"Of course I do. But I'm finally feeling better, and I'm worried that if I talk to him, or if I email him and he responds, it'll take me back to that awful place. I don't want to get caught up in all of that again."

"Well, I still want to kill him," Farah said. "If I ever see him his scrotum will not survive intact."

"Is the Hijabi Renegade allowed to touch balls?" I asked.

She grinned. "You haven't heard the hadith? And the Prophet said, 'Women should refrain from touching the balls of anyone but their husbands and infants, unless the owner of the balls hurts your best friend, in which case it is permissible to kick them, hard, with your steel-toed boots.'"

"So that's what the Prophet would do. Fine. If you ever run into Jamie, you have my permission to kick him in the nuts."

"You are so kind," Farah said. "Now will you please let me repack that suitcase? It looks like it threw up."

"You and my mother. Go ahead."

We switched places; I lay on the bed while she kneeled in front of the shiny blue suitcase I'd bought from Target. My mother had gone with me and turned teary-eyed from the mere sight of the luggage display.

"You know, that could be a great song," she said as she organized my clothes into piles.

"What?"

"What would the Prophet do? Like . . ." She started snapping her fingers, pumping her arm in the air. "*What would the Prophet do, yeah yeah, what would the Prophet do? Would he kick you in the balls would he catch you when you fall would he send Ali with a sword would he just look really bored* . . . Wow, that wasn't bad for extemporaneous lyrics."

"You're so dumb."

"If by dumb you mean Harvard-bound genius, then yes, I concur. Qureshi, this deranged mouse T-shirt is pretty ugh."

"It's a deranged bear. Radiohead's *Kid A* album."

"I thought that was your least favorite album."

"My least favorite of the most awesome albums of all time, you mean. God, you know what sucks? 'Let Down' was my favorite song, and then Jamie went and made it our song, and now I can't listen to it because it makes me sad."

"No, what sucks the most is the fact he tried to cheat on you with your BFF," Farah reminded me.

"Yeah, that too." I hung upside down, enjoying the blood rush to my head. "Can I tell you something?"

"Whenever you say that it means I won't like it, but yes, go ahead."

"I know I'm supposed to hate him, and I do, but sometimes I remember how nice he could be, how nice it was to be with him."

"Wait. Mr. Milan Kundera has something to say about this." Farah toyed with her phone, looking up the quote. "'In the sunset of dissolution, everything is illuminated by the aura of nostalgia, even the guillotine.'"

"Okay, I see Mr. Kundera's point, but it's not like I'm waxing nostalgic about the guillotine," I argued. "Like, whenever we hooked up, he was so considerate, and sensitive—if I ever felt self-conscious, or nervous, he'd totally sense it, and stop and ask me if what we were doing was okay. He was so good like that, he never forced me or pressured me. I mean, compared to a guy like Ryan—"

"Qureshi, stop," Farah said, holding up her hand. "Listen to yourself. You're giving Jamie a pass because he'd never insult you to your face like Ryan!"

"That's not what I said," I protested.

"The fact you're even using Ryan as a comparison—that's why guys get away with being shitheads, because their baseline is so goddamn low, even lower if they're cute. Oh, you'd never date rape me? Awesome! Oh, you actually listened to something I said without talking over me? You're such a great guy! It's bullshit."

"My T-shirt," I said, gesturing at the *Kid A* T-shirt now bunched into a ball in her fist.

"Do you know my mother makes my five-year-old sister set the table for dinner, and do you know what my eight-year-old brother does? Sits there and plays video games until it's time to eat."

"What does that have to do with anything?" I asked.

"It has everything to do with everything!"

"I'm pretty sure Jamie's mother made him set the table," I said. "And my point is it could have been worse. He could have been a dick *and* bad in bed. He could have been a dick *and* not taken me to the Theater of Dreams. It's like you said, no one's all good and all bad."

As Farah groaned and hurled a pile of underwear at my head, my phone buzzed.

"Can you get that?" I asked. "It's next to the suitcase."

Farah retrieved my phone, her mouth dropping open. "You're *kidding* me."

"What?" I demanded.

"It's him."

"Jamie? Let me see."

He'd sent a photo of a pie, chocolate pecan from the looks of it. Hey Morning Dew made this and thought of you xx

xx. xx! The nerve of him, to write me so cavalierly, like he hadn't done the worst thing ever. The anger I'd assumed had faded had only gone dormant, and now it erupted, until all I saw was red.

"I'm going to kill him!" I said.

"What are you doing?" Farah asked.

"I'm calling him."

"But you said—"

"Shut up, it's on speaker."

Jamie's phone rang once, twice.

Thrice.

"Hello there."

It'd been so long since I'd heard his voice outside of my own head. I wasn't prepared for what it would feel like, an electric lightning bolt from ear to heart.

"Morning Dew?" he said.

"Hi," I said.

"Hey. It's nice to hear your voice."

He sounded like he meant it. But then he always did. In

spite of what I now knew, I could feel a part of myself still drawn to him, still yearning, wishing things had turned out differently.

Dammit.

"How are you?" he asked.

I tried not to look at Farah, who had grabbed Big Muchli and was mock punching him in the face to demonstrate what I ought to do next.

But I didn't want to punch him. I wanted to cry. Calling him had been a mistake.

"I'm good," I said. "What about you?"

"I've been better," Jamie said, which wasn't his usual MO.

"What's the matter?"

A frustrated Farah threw Big Muchli in the air.

"Aunt Marianne left for Brazil."

"Oh?" I said. "But I'm sure she'll have a good time."

"She has lung cancer."

"Oh. I didn't know she smoked."

"She doesn't. She never did."

"Shit. I'm so sorry. She's really special."

On the floor below, Farah rolled her eyes and started playing an imaginary violin.

"Hold on a sec, Jamie." I took it off speaker, covered the mouthpiece. "Jesus, Farah, his aunt has cancer!"

"So what! That doesn't change what he did!" Farah exclaimed.

I put it back on speaker. "Jamie?"

"Yeah?"

"I wanted to say . . ." What did I want to say? There'd been days when I'd spent hours imagining exactly this moment, and now that it was here, I was without words.

"Goddammit!" Farah cried. "Jamie, it's Farah."

"Oh, hey, Farah!" Jamie said. "How are you?"

No hint of fear, or remorse, or even hesitation.

We looked at each other. Unbelievable. I nodded at Farah. Go.

"You know, it's funny you called, because Qureshi and I were just talking about you," she said.

"Oh yeah?"

"Yeah. We were talking about how you're a two-faced lying scumbag, who thought you almost got away with trying to kiss me. What did you think, that I wouldn't say anything? Well, maybe you've gotten away with this in the past, but both Q and I see you for what you are, which is a lame, duplicitous, manipulative loser."

"Ouch," Jamie said.

"Ouch?" I said. "That's all you have to say?"

"What can I say?"

At least he had the decency not to deny it. "I don't know, Jamie," I responded. "That you're sorry?"

"I never wanted to hurt either of you. You're both such amazing women."

Farah seemed like she was about to blow again, and I gave

her a warning look. I wanted to hear how he was going to justify his behavior.

"So you think it's okay that you tried to kiss Farah?" I said.

"Nah, I know that wasn't cool. I got caught up in the moment."

"She's my *best friend*," I said, suddenly sounding wretched.

"And I'm still her best friend," Farah cried. "And I will kill you if I ever see you."

"Whoa," Jamie said. "You two make a fearsome pair."

How could this be? Even after being exposed as a liar, he was trying to be charming.

"Unbelievable," Farah said.

"Listen, I'm not proud of what I did. But I really did like you, Morning Dew. I think you're such a beautiful—"

"Stop it!" I said. "It doesn't matter anymore, what you think. I trusted you with my heart, but you didn't deserve it. I don't need you to feel good about myself. I'm sorry about Aunt Marianne, but I don't want to have anything to do with you. Shame on you, Jamie. Never contact me again."

I hung up before he could reply. My hands were shaking.

Farah embraced me.

"That was awesome!" she said. "You totally gave it to him. I'm so proud of you. You did it, Qureshi!"

"I know," I said. "I know!"

I wasn't sure who yelled first, Farah or me, but soon we were both screaming and stamping our feet and jumping up and down until we collapsed on the bed.

"By the way, this whole time you've had underwear on your head," Farah told me.

As I yanked it from my curls, I was still laughing, but then I realized it was the same pair I'd worn to the Theater of Dreams, and started to cry.

Thirty-Two

THE CONVERSATION WITH JAMIE sent me into a downward spiral, but I recovered more quickly this time. Talking to him had given me some closure, and helped me realize that I could, and would, move on. A lot of things were changing; my parents had gone on two date nights, including a Bollywood film where my father had managed to stay awake past intermission. I'd sent them to our local Italian restaurant for a dinner date with my pie wallah money. I'd even caught my mother coming out of my father's study twice. Once, when I entered the kitchen, they'd stopped talking, like they'd been sharing a confidence, and it was nice to feel excluded, like they were beginning to have a life without me.

But I was realistic. My father was still self-involved and a terrible conversationalist, but at least he was trying, which was more than he'd ever done before.

Farah left for Harvard and was already sending me emails about the cool people she was meeting, Muslim and otherwise, and how she'd discovered a great music venue called, wait for it, The Middle East. Since I don't pray, I wrote, *would you include Aunt Marianne in your prayers? Sure*, she wrote back, *I can pray for her when I say du'a, but you should also send her good vibes*. So I did.

The day before I left for Penn, two things happened.

I was able to listen to "Let Down" without crying, and my father actually came to my room.

"All ready to go?" he said.

"Almost."

He appraised my luggage. "Can you fit one more thing?"

"Depends on how big it is."

"Not big. A gift for your birthday."

My birthday wasn't until tomorrow, but I was impressed he'd gotten it almost right. "A birthday gift? For me?"

"For you." He revealed what he'd been concealing behind his back: a red hardcover book, with one word on the front—*Poetry*.

I opened it. On the first page was an inscription.

To Shabnam,

May You Always Find Solace in Poetry

Love, Dad

"Did you make this?" I asked.

"Yes," my father said. "It is a selection of my favorite

poems—on the left is the Urdu, transliterated into English, on the right my translation. Almost all of the poems that have meant the most to me are contained inside. Your mother put the book together using a website."

So that was why they'd been acting conspiratorial.

"This is so awesome." I hugged him. "Thanks, Dad. If you don't mind, I'll ask Mom to order another copy and send it to Chotay Dada in Pakistan."

"Is Chotay Dada interested in poetry?" my father asked.

"I don't know. But maybe it will give him solace, too."

"Poetry can give everyone solace," my father agreed, "if they are open to it."

"So you know they teach Urdu at Penn," I said. "I was thinking I'd study it, and maybe one day I'd be good enough to read Faiz in the original. Maybe even Ghalib, too."

You know the look fathers have when they're walking their daughters down the aisle to get married? That was what my father looked like when I told him this, all sentimental, and proud.

My father nodded. "I'd like that. I wish you all the best, *beta*. I wish you all the happiness in the world."

"I love you," I said. I couldn't remember the last time I'd told him this, or if I'd ever told him this.

"Yes," my father said.

I laughed. "By yes you mean, I love you too?"

"Yes," he replied. "That is what I mean."

I stayed up late that night, reading my father's favorite poems.

And if you want to know what happened next, it goes something like this:

The nightingale, she said farewell to the rose. She nursed her wounded heart, she brought her loved ones close. She spread her wings. She left the garden.

She flew.

A NOTE ON PARTITION

As Mr. Blake tells his class, the Partition of India in 1947 was the largest mass migration in human history, with an estimated fourteen million people displaced and hundreds of thousands killed. It was a violent, traumatic event, a disastrous culmination of centuries of colonial oppression, a deep, dark wound in the psyche of the subcontinent to which there are no public memorials, and, until recently, no museums. It is an event many have tried to forget, even as its aftereffects continue to this day.

People who were teenagers during Partition are now in their eighties, and many of their stories remain untold. The 1947 Partition Archive is a nonprofit organization dedicated to recording and preserving eyewitness accounts of Partition from the remaining survivors, so that their stories are remembered and known. You can find out more, including how to become a citizen historian, on their website, www.1947partitionarchive.org.

In October 2016, the world's first Partition Museum opened in Amritsar, India, dedicated to the victims, survivors, and legacy of Partition. Learn more at www.partitionmuseum.org.

A NOTE ON FAIZ AHMED FAIZ

Faiz Ahmed Faiz was one of thc great modern Urdu poets. Since his death in 1984, his work has continued to move and inspire readers throughout the world. His poems have been widely translated into English. If you'd like to read more by him, one book I highly recommend is *The Rebel's Silhouette: Selected Poems by Faiz Ahmed Faiz*, translated by the poet Agha Shahid Ali.

ACKNOWLEDGMENTS

My deep gratitude to the following for making this book possible:

To my agent, Ayesha Pande, for her years of guidance and support, and for being a champion of diversity in publishing.

To my editor, Rosemary Brosnan, and the fantastic team at HarperTeen, for seeing the heart of this book and helping make it come alive.

To Venk Kandadai, for sharing his passion for Radiohead's music.

To the Faiz Foundation Trust for permission to publish Faiz's work, and to Nicky Dodd for being my woman on the ground.

To the Vanderbilt University MSA crew: Merna El-Rifai, Sumaiya Delane, Safiah Hassan, Dini Muniro, Bushra Rahman and Hamzah Raza, for sharing their thoughts and stories with me.

And to my beloveds, Anand and Lillah, in whom my heart has found a home.